BITTEN

Book Four of the Stanley Cooper Chronicles

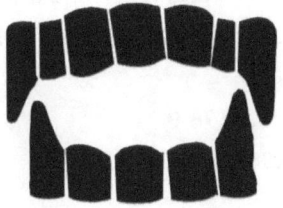

Scott A. Johnson

ISBN-13: 978-0-578-53196-0
ISBN-10: 0-578-53196-8

Edited by Lily K. Coy-Johnson

Printed in the USA

First Edition

This book is dedicated to the person who gave me back my life and made me feel like me again. Thank you, Katie. Without you this book wouldn't exist.

This book is dedicated to the person who gave me back my life and made me feel like me again. Thank you, Katie. Without you this book wouldn't exist.

THE AUTHOR WOULD LIKE TO THANK

The usual cast of miscreants, you know who you are.
Clint, Heather, Hadley, Callum, and Corbin
Matt and Meg
Anna and Zoe
Nikki, Ward, Wes, and Jake
Kristin and Jarred
Nicole, Mike, Al, Paul, Anne, and Lucy
Gary and Tim
Marisa and James
Suz and Bill
Symantha and Anna L.
The Vampire Court of Austin
Max, Taco, Buster, Bitsy, Fuzz-Butt, and Timoune
To everyone who believes in me
To everyone who reads Stanley's Adventures...

THANK YOU

1

Pittsburgh slept. Well, it never really slept. The good and decent people stayed in their homes after a certain hour while the unsavory things came out of theirs and stalked the streets. The only things left in the dark were those too stupid to stay indoors, or those who went out looking for trouble. And trouble went by many names. For some, it was "a good time." For others, it was "adventure." For many, it was "just a few drinks." Whatever. The bottom line was that at the end of the night, when the sun came up, people paid the price for their troubles, and people who lived in Pittsburgh were often glad to pony up.

Night, for whatever reason, attracted a short list of characters. The young, the brave, the foolish. They went to their clubs or bars, wandered the streets looking for the things that only came out at night. The absence of daylight made the ghoulies and ghosties and long-legged beasties come out to play.

At least, that's what people thought. The truth behind the

whole "monsters come out in the dark" bit was because most "monsters" had day jobs, many of them in civil service. But that didn't stop certain brave or desperate souls from wandering about in search of proof of the afterlife.

We all cling to the desperate notion that, once our bodies stop working, we continue on in some other plane of existence. Whether people call it paranormal, preternatural, or some other weirdo label, it always comes down to the same thing. People want to believe that the physical realm they live in isn't all there is to the world. It's a desperate need for some people, to live with hope that when the end comes, it isn't really the end. It's actually the basis for every religion. And yet, for some people, the notion of ghosts or phantoms is ludicrous. It's difficult to explain, and harder still to understand. But psychics, frauds and real ones, often make their livings on the sliver of doubt that exists between heaven and the haunted mansion.

Real psychics like me.

Fakes like the joker that sat across the table in the darkened basement of his home in West End. He called himself Radu, after the brother of Vlad the Impaler from Romanian history. His real name was Bradley.

"All join hands," he said in a thick, most likely fake, Russian accent. "The spirits are with us tonight."

All twelve people in attendance, plus the goofball in the

turban, linked hands and waited for further instruction. It was a good con. The energy of the room leaped by several degrees with every hand linked, and every person's will power combined to help bridge the gap between the living and the dead. Or would have, if "Bradu" had any ability whatsoever. Which he didn't.

There was, however, one ghost present. One I invited. He stood behind Bradu and snickered.

"Can you believe this guy?"

Doug Appel was a Pittsburgh cop, tough as nails, no-nonsense, and eager to put the hurt on bad guys. Of course, that was when he was alive. A severe car crash caused by some unsavory types had relieved him of the burden of his life, but not the thirst for justice.

And I was the only one in the room who could see or hear him.

"There's a button under the table," said Appel. "Goes to a piston under one of the legs. The whole room is wired with speakers. This guy put some serious effort into this shit."

Bradu's head lolled back as he growled deep in his throat. The lights flickered a bit, no doubt from another electronic device secreted somewhere in the room, and he thrashed a bit, then he threw his head upright and stared at us all with buggy eyes.

"Who... summons... me..?"

The voice that came out of him was somewhere between a

two-pack-a-day smoker and an asthmatic pre-teen.

"We ask your guidance," said the group's chairwoman, who also happened to be my client. "Grant us knowledge from beyond the grave."

"Speak... your... question," said Bradu.

I gave Appel a silent cue and he vanished.

"I need to speak to my husband," said another woman. "I need to know if he's all right."

Bradu dropped his head for a moment, then raised it again. His eyes were closed, and the raspy voice was gone in favor of a more somber tone.

"Hello, Helen," he said.

"Murray?" Tears ran down Helen's face at the possibility of talking to her dead husband again.

"Yes, Helen," he said. "It's me. I'm fine. Heaven is nice."

I bristled.

When people die and come back, they love to spin yarns about dead relatives and harps and clouds and all the wonderful things religions tell them about what "heaven" is supposed to be like, and it's all a great comfort.

When I died, I saw nothing. Bubkes. A great void of black that stretched out from the moment my back hit the concrete until I woke up on a gurney. Every notion I had about an afterlife changed. Then I started to see dead people everywhere I went,

4

and those notions changed again.

"Tell me again, how much money did you pay this guy?" I whispered to my client.

"Five thousand. Apiece."

I shook my head.

Bradu collapsed in mock-exhaustion from "channeling" Helen's husband, then panted as he sat up.

"I sense there are those among us who do not believe in my powers," he said. "I shall now demonstrate my connection with the afterlife."

Bradu closed his eyes and breathed deeply. As he did, the table rose off the floor to the delight of almost everyone in the room. As it slammed up and down, the lights flickered a bit more and whispers came from seemingly nowhere. A couple of the women squealed. The men shrank into their chairs. The guy knew how to lay it on thick and commit to a role.

Appel reappeared with a grin on his ethereal face.

Showtime.

I mimicked his head-lolling antics and shook with as much violence as I could muster without falling out of my chair. When I snapped my head up, Bradu sat with his eyes fixed on me.

"Sorry," I said. "Your schtick put me into seizures."

"How dare you!"

"Save it," I said as I got up. "Electronic gizmos, speaker

wire, it all boils down to one thing. Bullshit. You're a fraud."

"But he knew about my husband," said Helen.

"So does anyone who reads the paper," I said. "I'm sorry, folks, but this guy is a complete fake."

"There's always a skeptic in the crowd," said Bradu. "But my gifts are unique! I can communicate with the dead... "

"I'm not a skeptic," I said. "I know you're a fake because I really can talk to the dead. Her husband's not here. The only thing here is your greed, you parasite."

"How do we know *you're* not the fake," he said, "here to try to trample over my legitimate business?"

It was the opening I hoped for.

"I'm the fake? Really? Boys?"

The lights snapped out. A green glow erupted from the center of the table.

"You dare to call me a fake?" He wasn't the only one who could lay it on thick.

From out of the glow stepped figures, wraiths of terrible origin. Three of them, to be precise. The first was Appel, his ghostly body a bloody reminder of the accident that claimed his life. The second, a full-fledged demon, red with a wicked smile and eyes that burned through the souls of those stupid enough to stare into them. The third apparition was the most terrifying of the group, the most frightening thing I could imagine: a headless clown.

Bradu toppled backward and cowered behind his chair as the three wraiths closed in around him.

"No!" The accent disappeared along with his composure. "For fuck's sake! Please! No! Get them away!"

"The dead don't like it when con-men take advantage of the living!" I gave my most menacing stare, which, to be fair, was about as intimidating as a pug watching a cheeseburger.

"Get them away!" Bradu lunged backward and came up with a gun in his hand, which he pointed at Stephanie, my client. "I mean it! Get them away!"

By nature, I'm not a violent man. True, things happen to me that are pretty weird, and I do occasionally have to get my hands dirty, so to speak. But there comes a point when even the most gentle person reaches his limit. When all good intention goes out the window and all that's left is rage.

Something snapped inside of me.

I stormed toward Bradu, eyes locked on his. His expression changed from garden-variety fear to one of abject terror, and he shifted his aim toward me. I didn't care. I snatched the gun away, then backhanded him with it. As he lay on the floor, I crouched over his trembling body.

"You son of a bitch," I growled. "Preying on the innocent, the bereaved, the desperate. You want to know what it's like to lose everything? You want to know what it feels like to want so bad to talk to a dead loved one that you'd even go to a douchebag like you?"

"Hey... Stan..." Appel crouched beside me, but I didn't care.

"You want to know what it's like to feel the pain of dying? Or how about the pain of having to live when everyone you love is dead?"

My face was inches from his, so close he could probably smell the tuna sandwich I had for dinner. I wanted so badly to let loose just a fraction of the energy I held inside myself, to make him feel my rage, my pain. To burn out the circuitry of his mind with every agonizing moment of my life.

But I couldn't.

"Back down," said Kevin's head. His body held it out to me. "He's scared plenty, okay? We'll take it from here."

I dropped the gun and stood up. The little puke looked like a child afraid of his father.

"I hear of you again..." I left the threat to hang in the wind. Truth was, I couldn't think of anything appropriately terrifying. But Bradu's imagination would do the job for me.

"Oh my God," said Stephanie. "He could've killed me. Thank you, Mister Cooper."

"Whatever," I said.

"He could've shot you."

"Yeah," I said. "How 'bout that?"

I wouldn't really have cared if he did. After all, I didn't have anything left to live for.

2

Once upon a time, I believed in happy endings. The good guy got the girl, the bad guy always got his comeuppance, and everyone lived happily ever after. I always believed that, if I did enough good, good things would happen.

In some parts of the world, they call it "karma," and it works kind of like a reward from some great invisible whatsit in the sky that keeps score.

My mother used to tell me that every hardship was a jewel in my crown when I got to heaven. Then I grew up. I died and discovered there was no heaven. I came back into a world that didn't understand me and didn't care. I retreated from everyone and everything as a method of self-preservation until I met one beautiful person. That person made me believe again that I could be loved, that maybe there was some higher power. Maybe she was my reward for trying to be a good person all my life. But then…

Maggie died in childbirth. There. I said it.

Our lives were supposed to be lived together. We were supposed to grow old together, live out our golden years in our weird little shop with our weird little friends. We were supposed to live in our apartment together and raise our baby together. But things didn't work out the way we planned.

Things never go according to plan.

No happy endings for Stanley Cooper.

She used to taunt me, tell me that the way I ate, the risks I took, she'd outlive me. She should've outlived me.

I sat in my apartment and wished I could feel. As deep as I loved her, I thought I would cry, scream, curse God or whatever giant invisible whatsit sat out there in the great beyond for taking her from me. But all I felt was numb. All I had in me was a whole lot of nothing. I couldn't cry anymore. I couldn't be angry, or sad. I just... was. Maybe it was the place.

My apartment didn't have any reminders of Maggie. The space we shared was across Pittsburgh on Carson Street, just above her little shop of curious things. Which was why I wasn't there. I couldn't be. Not yet. Our friend, Andi, was a more-than-capable shopkeeper. After all, she was its mother.

When I moved over to Maggie's apartment, I kept my own place. I wasn't sure why at the time, other than it made for a convenient place to store cursed things. But as I sat on the couch,

12

watched the dust motes drift through sunbeams, I was almost glad I did. Over there, I half-expected to see Maggie walk out of the bedroom or stand outside the shop door.

It wouldn't be all that strange. I do see ghosts.

But hers was the only one I really wanted to see. And hers was the one that I didn't.

I watched for months as she withered away. Every day, I shifted my Sight, watched the struggle inside her, but there was always hope. Even on her last day, I thought maybe she might pull through. Of course, I was wrong. The baby was too strong.

It was the baby that killed her. Rather, it was the demon that fought for control of its soul that killed her. Every day, our baby grew stronger. Every day, Maggie grew weaker.

I tried to convince her to terminate the pregnancy, but she wouldn't hear of it. My argument even resulted in a few uncomfortable nights spent in the old apartment. But every day, an epic battle played out, and since I was the only one who could see it, I was the only one who knew what was really going on.

Our baby was strong, more so than any living creature. The light that shone out of Maggie's belly hurt to look at, radiated off of her in waves. White, pure, beautiful. But beneath that beautiful white, sick oily black swirled and stained our baby's soul. Maggie fought it, fed the baby her own energies. She made our baby strong enough to fight the darkness, but at a cost. The more she gave, the more the baby took, until there was nothing left to give. Then she gave more.

She dropped so much weight. Her beautiful curves turned to bony hips and ribs, a spine that protruded from her back, and sunken cheeks. Her eyes never changed, though. Always bright. Always full of life and joy. Always fierce. The love she felt for our unborn child was the kind fairy tale mothers felt. Eternal. Limitless.

The day my son was born, Maggie's body gave out. She lived just long enough to hear his first cry, feel his warmth on her breast, and smile. Then she looked at me, closed her eyes, and was gone.

I wept for days. I didn't know a human being could cry so much that they felt empty, but I sat on the floor in our apartment, cored. I was nothing. Andi cared for the baby while I was busy feeling sorry for myself. It was two days before I even knew if it was a boy or girl. When the day came, I had a son. A baby boy. My dream come true, and a nightmare all the same.

I named him Daniel, Maggie's wish. Then I left. It wasn't the most responsible thing to do, but I couldn't look at him. In my head, I still saw the oil slick of filth that tore Maggie apart. I couldn't look at him without the thought that he took her away from me. So I left him in the capable hands of his aunt Andi and my overbearing mother, in the safest place I knew in Pittsburgh:

The shop.

Air swirled as the disused air conditioner came on and sent the dust into rolling patterns of chaos. Water dripped off the bottle in my hand as I raised it to my lips and took another comfortable swallow of lager.

There were no reminders of her. And because there were none, I missed her even more.

The second bedroom door rattled. Someone who didn't know what lay behind the door would attribute it to the air conditioner, but I knew better.

"You can't come out," I said. "Go fuck yourself."

The rattle stopped. Stupid doll. If I had a dollar for every time I came home and found it out of place, I could probably afford a pretty nice dinner at Primanti Brothers. For two.

Damn it.

Unlike the rest of Pittsburgh, Carson Street slept for no one. No matter the time of day, something moved and hustled. Objects were sold or bought. Even in the wake of the passing of one of its most beloved merchants, commerce continued. Cars still puttered along, pedestrians still hurried to and from shops to spend their money, and the scent of soup and gyros still wafted through the air like temptresses. Life went on, despite how much I wanted it to stop.

I stood across the street and stared at the darkened window that was Maggie's shop. Everything about it looked the same as it did a month ago, a year ago, but there was something about it that seemed colder. Sadder. Maybe I was projecting, but because I knew she wasn't there, the whole place just didn't seem right. I needed to go in, needed to own up to my responsibilities and get back to work. I needed to see my son and make sure the demon that killed Maggie was not in permanent residence in his soul.

And if it was? What then?

I needed to, but I didn't want to. I didn't want to see the shop without her, or open the door and not see her smile as she bounced toward me. I didn't want to endure the pitying looks or empathy, didn't want to try to console a building the size of a city block. I didn't even know how.

My father's words came back to me.

Hitch up your britches and get it done, son. That's what being a grown-up is all about.

I took a deep breath, looked both ways, and headed across the street.

No fewer than a dozen faces looked up as the bell over the door tinkled to herald my arrival. Of them, I recognized two. The rest turned misty eyes and sympathetic looks my direction, then took slow shuffling steps to offer their condolences. The urge to turn and walk back out the door was strong.

"How are you, baby?" My mother waddled across the room, in a way that was both patronizing and emasculating. She put her arms around me and hugged me tight into the crinkle of her windbreaker.

"Holding up," I said with a forced smile. "Where's Daniel?"

"Little dear," she said. "He's in the back. I set up your old bassinet for him."

"You still have that thing?"

"Of course." She looked wounded. "I would never throw something so precious out."

This from the woman who tried to have me committed.

I wove through well-wishers and handshakes, hugs and shoulder-grabs until I made it to the back counter. Andi's tear-stained face looked up from behind the register. She forced a smile.

"I'm sorry," I said. "I didn't mean..."

"No worries. You needed time."

"It wasn't fair," I said. "And it's time I started acting like a father."

Andi nodded and gestured toward the back.

"Go see your son, then," she said. "Dad."

The word stung more than I thought it would. I never pictured myself as a dad, much less a single parent. But she was right. Daniel was a responsibility I had shirked for too long. I took a deep breath and stepped to the back of the shop.

One of the advantages of taking up residence in a living building is that, no matter what, whoever is in the building is never alone. The same advantage can turn awkward for showers and bathroom visits, but in the case of a baby, it's like having the world's largest nanny.

The crib sat at the center of the brass inlaid pentacle that dominated the floor. It wasn't so long ago that human rats had torn it out, but Maggie loved it, used it often, so the question of whether or not to have it repaired never came up. As an added bonus, Andi knew how to make certain that nothing that sat in the center of the star could ever come to harm.

While the lights in the rest of the room blazed at full brightness, those over the crib softened and dimmed. A warm breeze blew under the crib while a cool one floated over the top.

The bassinet looked terrifying in the center of the circle, like something out of a 1970s-era horror movie. But as I approached, I was more surprised by how clean it was, how immaculate my mother had kept it. The white wicker showed very little dust, and none of the reeds were split or broken. I never knew she took such care of it.

Daniel lay wrapped in a blue blanket, wide awake, eyes open. As I peered over the side, I expected him to see me and cry at the scars on my face, my mangled arm, or at least for him to not know who I was. But he smiled and let out a tiny baby giggle.

My heart melted. All the fear and trepidation I had about our first meeting slid out of my mind on greased wheels. I didn't need to shift my Sight to look into his soul. It was written on his face. He wasn't a demon. Daniel was my son. He was our son. Maggie's and mine. He was a living piece of her, like she hadn't really left me.

I scooped him up with my good arm and stared into his eyes, then I hugged him close. Daniel snuggled my neck and cooed. I sank to my knees and cried.

"Maggie... look what we made. Look at our son. Look at how beautiful. Oh, gods... Look at how beautiful."

Andi stepped through the curtain and found me in Maggie's old rocking chair with Daniel in my arms, a bottle in his mouth.

"It's closing time," she said. "I can take him upstairs and... "

"No," I said. "It's fine. I've got him."

She stopped and looked unsure.

"You need a night out," I said. "You've done more than your share of work with him, and I can't even begin to thank you. He's my kid, and I need to start acting like a father. You go out and have fun tonight."

19

"But what if..?"

"I've got my mother to help me if I need it," I said.

"Are you sure?"

I'd rather have my toenails torn off with rusty pliers than call my mother for anything, but backup is backup.

"Absolutely," I said. "Go."

Andi skipped across the room and kissed me on the cheek, then leaned down and gave Daniel a gentle kiss on the forehead.

"Goddess watch over him," she said as she traced the sign of the pentacle on his forehead with her finger.

"Go," I said. "Before I come to my senses."

Andi bounded out the back door just as my mother came through the curtain.

"Where's she going?"

"Out," I said. "She deserves it."

"But what about..?"

"For crying out loud, Ma! Don't you think I can take care of a baby for an evening?"

Mom scanned me up and down, then put her hands on her hips.

"No," she said. "Come on. I'll help you give him his bath and put him down."

3

A long time ago, I came to grips with the weirdness that surrounds my life. Most people have friends, a nine-to-five job, a couple of kids, and a mortgage. They don't usually have monsters that attack, demons at the door, and ghosts that stand around and gawk at them. Most of them also don't make their homes in a living storefront that sells witchcraft supplies. And, to my knowledge, the majority of them haven't died, or if they have, they generally stayed that way.

I'm not normal.

Actually, I'm about four blocks and a long bus ride from normal. It's not at all uncommon, for example, for nasty critters to attack me. It's how my arm went from being a useful part of my anatomical society to a burned, grotesque, non-functional appendage. It's also how I lost my friend, Taylor, and, in a roundabout way, Maggie.

I sat on the couch with Bitsy, the cat who knew more than

she let on, in my lap. Her emerald eyes shone in the candlelight while I sipped my rum and Coke. When I stopped petting her to take a drink, she headbutted my hand.

"I know," I said. "I miss her too."

"Little dear." My mother came from the bedroom and closed the door. "He never puts up a fuss when I put him to bed. Not like you at all."

"Please don't start," I said.

"You used to pitch such a fit! It used to take the patience of Job to get you to even take a nap. And when you got older, you always complained it was hot or too cold in the house. Not like this place. Always seems to be the perfect temperature."

Mom still didn't quite get that the house was alive. I'd told her more than once, so on some level she knew it, but she couldn't reconcile it in her own world where spooky stuff just didn't happen. My world terrified her, so she coped in the only way she could. Denial.

"Weird how that happens," I said as I raised my glass for another sip.

As the glass touched my lips, the room went cold. Bitsy stood and arched her back, fur raised. Even Mom felt the shift, and for a moment, terror replaced her overbearing expression. The stairwell echoed with heavy footsteps. Nothing dangerous could approach the apartment, the shop saw to it. But whatever came up the stairs was enough to cause every nerve in my body to ignite at the same time.

A slow thud hit the door once, twice, then a third, followed by what sounded like something sliding down the face. I glanced at the clock. It was after eleven at night. Nothing wholesome ever happened on Carson Street after ten.

Bitsy sprang to the floor and scampered into Daniel's room as I got up and edged toward the door.

"No," said my mother. "Don't answer it."

"Someone might be in trouble."

"You are a father now! You can't go putting yourself in danger anymore! Think about your son!"

"I am," I said, as I took a deep breath and opened the door.

Andi fell into the apartment, her knuckles bloody, her clothing torn. Someone did a real number on her, beat her, bloodied her. So she came to the safest place she knew.

"Mom! Help!"

I looped my good arm under her and dragged her in, then closed and locked the door behind her.

"Andi? Andi... What happened? Andi, c'mon, tell me what happened. Who did this?"

Oh Gods... Not her... not her too. Gods, no. I can't lose her too. Not tonight. Not now. I can't lose her too.

Her eyes fluttered open for a moment, although they

23

didn't focus.

"Stan... " Her eyes closed again and she slumped.

"Shit... No... Andi!"

"I'm calling an ambulance!" Mom stabbed buttons on her cellphone and babbled at the attendant who answered. I didn't hear. I wasn't listening. I sat with Andi's head in my lap and stroked her hair.

"Don't you leave me," I whispered into her ear. "Don't you leave me, too..."

I try to avoid hospitals. It isn't that I have anything against the staff or doctors, it's just that I tend to spend too much time in the emergency room. And, usually, it's because I've either died or come damned close. Again.

But as I sat in the lobby, I was thankful for Mercy Hospital. Not only were they the ones who brought me back when I died, they were the doctors who put me back together when my arm exploded from the inside out. With the exception of an orderly or two, the place had a real top-notch staff.

Mom stayed behind with Daniel, which made things easier for me. She didn't like the "spooky" side of what I did, and I didn't want to hear her preach when I went to the chapel.

For lots of people, a near-death experience triggers a resurgence in religion, or a need to believe in something that's bigger than themselves. They need to have some sort of coping mechanism in their lives to deal with what happened to them, and that they came back from what most people consider the last big step in life.

I didn't find religion. In fact, any trace of religious thoughts were wiped away when I came back from the other side with a gloomy outlook of a big black nothing. No choirs of angels, no bright light, no dead relatives. Just darkness. The void. When that happened, my churchgoing days ended. But the chapel was the only place I knew where I could find someone who could keep me informed better than the overworked ER nurses.

"Barney?" I whispered. "You here?"

"Of course I am," he said. "I'm always around."

Barney stood up from a bench in such a way that I couldn't be sure if he'd been there before he spoke or not. He looked like he always did, in coveralls with a Pirates ball cap. His salt-and-pepper hair and kind face put everyone he appeared to at ease. Useful for a ghost. Or an angel. I wasn't sure which one he was, and he never admitted to anything.

"I brought someone in. A girl. She's in the ER. They're working on her. Could you..?"

"Back in a second." Barney shimmered and vanished. When he reappeared, his smile was replaced with concern.

"How is she?"

"Who did that to her?" He sounded angry. "What creature did that?"

"She got mugged..."

"That was no mugging," said the ghost. "She's in for a real fight. Something bit her. And whatever it was, it's infected her with darkness."

"What do you mean, bit her? Like, bit her?"

"Stanley," said Barney. "Tread lightly. I know what you've faced in the past, but... I wouldn't wish this on anyone." Before I could press him for more information, he faded like smoke.

"Thanks," I said as I left the chapel and hurried back to the ER waiting room. Every person who waited for attention had the same look of desperation, the same look of pain. One guy clutched a blood-soaked rag to his arm. On the other side of the room, a harried-looking woman tried to console a crying baby while her two other children gave in to boredom and ran around the room. There were more than thirty people in the waiting room, all of them with severe injuries, debilitating illnesses, and every one of them needed help.

And I didn't care about any of them.

As terrible as it may sound, at that moment, I didn't give a good God-damn about anyone in that room, because, to me, the only person that mattered was Andi.

It took me a few persuasive moments to get the admitting

nurse to buzz the door open, but in the end, I won out and made it back to see Andi. When I found her stall, I almost wished I'd stayed in the lobby.

A doctor and two nurses hovered around Andi's quiet body. Tubes ran up her nose and down her throat. More punctured the backs of her hands and her arms. I choked on a sob when I saw her.

"You shouldn't be back here," said a nurse. "We're doing the best we can, but you need to let us work."

"Please," I said. "I'm the only family she has left. Please help her."

The nurse's features softened.

"We'll do everything we can," she said. "Preliminary tests show some heavy blood loss, but I think we got her in time. She's going to be okay."

"Thank you." My lungs deflated and my knees went weak as my head spun with relief.

"I'll tell you one thing," said the nurse. "Your friend's one tough cookie. She put up a fight. We found skin and hair under her nails. Whoever did this to her didn't get away untouched. The police are on their way to take samples."

The nurses adjusted the side rails on the bed and pulled the bags off the IV tower and laid them across Andi's chest.

"Where are they taking her?"

"ICU," said the nurse. "It doesn't look like she needs sur-gery, but she's got a long night ahead of her."

"Can I come? I... I just don't want to let her out of my sight."

"No," said the nurse. "No visitors allowed in ICU at this time. You need to go home and get some rest."

"But—"

"Sir," she said with practiced kindness. "You did everything you could by bringing her here. But we've got her now. We'll do everything we can to take care of her. She's in good hands, okay? I promise."

I nodded in defeat.

"Do you want to take her belongings, or should we have them brought to her room?"

"No," I said. "I'll take them."

I stepped aside as they wheeled Andi's bed out of the stall and toward the elevator.

"We have your contact information, right? We'll get a room assignment for her and let you know what it is, Mister..?"

"Cooper," I said. "Just... keep her safe."

The bed disappeared around the corner toward the eleva-tor, and I was as alone as a person could be in a hospital emer-gency room. Andi's boots lay on the floor, next to her jacket. The skirt was in tatters as was her shirt and underthings. I didn't care about them, but the jacket was a gift from Maggie. It smelled of

28

clove cigarettes and sweat with just a hint of the original leather musk still evident. And the boots, Andi called her "ass-stompers" because of the huge sole and metal buckles that lined the upper part. Blood covered parts of the chrome and leather.

When Maggie died, I didn't want anything more to do with the paranormal world. Demons, zombies, witches and ghosts... So far as I cared they could all just find another clairvoyant to chase around. Too many people got hurt because I stuck my nose where it didn't belong. Too many people that I cared about.

And I'd be damned if I let Andi become another casualty.

I hurried out of the ER and headed back to the shop.

Mom stood as I came through the door.

"What happened? Is she all right? What did the doctors say?"

"She was attacked." I took Andi's boots to the kitchen and hung her coat on the rack by the door. "Wherever she was tonight, something there went after her. And I want to know what it was before it hurts someone else."

"You can't go running off like this anymore!" Mom stared at me through the kitchen pass-through. "You have a baby to think about! What's that little angel going to do if you go getting yourself killed chasing whatever did that to her? You've got to let this go and..."

"Mom!" My temper snapped like a dry twig. "I'm not just going to let anything go! How many people do I have to lose for you to see how important this is? How many weird things have to happen for you to admit it's all real? Magick, monsters, ghosts, demons... It's all real, and people are dying! I don't want to lose Andi, and someone has to stop whatever hurt her from hurting anyone else. What part of that don't you get?"

Mom gaped at me like a fish and sat on the couch. Tears welled in her eyes, and guilt slapped me in the back of the head.

"I just don't want to lose you," she said. "Not again."

My shoulders slumped as I felt all my righteous anger drain out into the floor. The buckles of Andi's boots glistened with red. Her blood. Her life. They were her favorite boots. They needed to be cleaned. She'd want them when she got out of the hospital. I took a sponge from under the counter and turned the water in the sink on cold.

"Honey." Mom's voice came from behind me. I didn't turn to look. I couldn't. "I made a lot of mistakes. When your father died, I didn't know how to handle anything. But this, your world, it scares me. Scares me bad. All I want is to be a good grandmother to your baby, but I don't want to lose you again."

"Was that why you tried to have me committed?"

There was no answer from behind me, and I fought the powerful urge to turn around so I could see her face.

"I didn't know what else to do." Her voice trembled, full of tears. I struck a nerve. "You were saying such scary stuff, I thought..."

"What? That calling me crazy was the right thing to do? You could've given me the benefit of the doubt."

Silence again.

"I'm sorry," she said, after a while. "I'm so sorry."

"I'll tell you the truth," I said as I scrubbed the buckles on Andi's boots clean. "Maggie called you. Maggie's the one who wanted you to be involved in Daniel's life. Not me. You didn't like her because she was a witch, but she was a better person than you gave her credit for. She was the one who wanted to give you the chance to be a grandmother. Not me."

Mom was quiet as she walked back into the living room, picked up her purse, and left.

I almost ran after her. Almost begged her to come back and act like a mom to me and a grandmother to Daniel. But in the end, I couldn't. I finished cleaning the blood off Andi's boots and set them beside the door to dry.

Her leather jacket looked rough, but then, it always did. Still, it needed some tender loving care, so I fished through the pockets to make sure nothing got ruined. In one pocket, I found a drink receipt. On it, in black and red lettering, days and hours were listed, as well as a time stamp of when the drink was sold. It fit the time frame. At the top, a single word, the club's name, the place she was when she was attacked.

Nocturnity.

The next day dragged by in a still-life of hospital rooms and vending machine snacks. Andi's doctors tried their best to assure me that she'd be all right, but their plastic faces and practiced smiles told me the same lies just before I lost Maggie.

Barney was a better resource. He eavesdropped on the doctors and nurses and reported back their official diagnosis of beats-the-shit-out-of-us. They gave her transfusion after transfusion, bag after bag of whole blood and plasma, but her body just devoured it, and hours later, she looked anemic again. They ran tests as they looked for hemorrhages or internal bleeding, but found nothing. When Barney told me the doctors wanted to do exploratory surgery, I knew they were at the end of their experience. I needed to take a good look at her in a way only I knew how, and I didn't want to do it.

Every natural thing has energy. Some call it a soul, others an aura, but it doesn't matter by what name it goes. The bottom line is, energy pulses through every natural thing in existence. Some people learn to manipulate that energy, and they call it Magick. People like me can see it, and use our knowledge and experience to figure things out.

Like what was wrong with a young woman in a hospital bed.

I lowered the walls of my perception, opened doorways in my mind, and let myself See the world as it really was. When I opened my eyes, the sterile white and beige room was no more, replaced by vibrant colors of energy that raced along pathways laid out in wires and tubes. Doctors passed with auras of blue and green, pink and yellow. The older doctors had brown splotches in theirs, memories of tragedies they had tried to repair and patients they had lost, no doubt. I didn't care about them. I turned my eyes toward Andi in her bed, and what I saw made me sick.

Andi's aura shone bright, shades of pink and white, power and purity that poured off her in waves of youthful exuberance that didn't always go right, but always had the best of intentions at heart. But her light was marred, broken by something that wasn't exactly the oil slick black I expected, but was more just an absence of light. Her own life force fought back hard against it, but something inside of her was just wrong. I closed the doors to my perception and turned away, unable to look at her without tears rolling down my cheeks.

"You see?" said Barney. "That's what I mean. She's infected. And this is darkness like you don't know."

"I'm not going to lose her, too." I stormed out of the hospital and headed back to the shop.

33

I called and apologized, so Mom came back, all smiles, like nothing happened. I knew her better, though. Mom never forgot anything. More, she saved up ammunition for when she needed to unleash a hellfire of guilt on her unsuspecting prey. She patted my arm and kissed my cheek, but experience told me she was just waiting for her chance.

The shop stayed closed for the day. Not great for business, but when the shop's mother lay in a hospital bed, no amount of reasoning seemed to help. The doors stayed closed up tight and the air inside grew thick with worry. I didn't care. I stood by the window in the kitchen and watched the sky, counted the hours and minutes until sundown while my mother doted over my son. When it came, I grabbed my jacket.

"Stay here," I said. "Watch over Daniel. Don't open the door for anyone." I turned and addressed the building. "You hear that? Anyone! I'll be back soon. You keep my mom and my son safe."

"It... It really is alive, isn't it?"

"She, mom. The building is a she. And, yes, she's alive. Andi brought her to life, and I think she's going to be pretty pissed if something happens to her mother."

"Can... Can I talk to it... her?"

"Knock yourself out," I said. "She likes it."

I crept into the bedroom where my son slept in his crib and stole what I hoped wouldn't be a last look at him.

"Maggie," I whispered. "If you're here, keep our son safe."

Maggie's pentacle necklace hung from the mirror in the bathroom. It wasn't my faith, but it felt right to wear it because it was hers, and it made me feel like she might be with me. Maggie had always given me strength, made me believe I could do more than I thought I could.

As I left the bedroom, I could almost see Maggie by the cradle, a look of concern on her face. It wasn't one of my ghost sightings, but just wishful thinking. Maggie wasn't around. If she were, she'd have shown herself.

"Back soon," I said as I hurried out the door to the stair-well. The door closed behind me and the deadbolt clicked into place.

BITTEN

4

Carson Street was home to every type of person anyone could imagine. Artists, collectors, chefs, and everything in between gathered in the little corner of Pittsburgh and forged a home for themselves. Every little shop had a story, and the proprietors were just as distinctive as the wares and services they sold. During the day, what passed for normal was decidedly odd, but in a freaky-fun way. At night, much of the "fun" dropped and many weird things came out of the shadows to bask in the moonlight.

Not to say Carson Street was a bad place at night. On the contrary, some of the more interesting things happened after the other shops locked their doors for the night. The weirdness just intensified, and for some, that meant danger. For others, it meant release.

The address on the receipt said the club wasn't too far from the shop, so I walked. Not that it was smart to be on foot at night, but I didn't like to drive much, and I was angrier than I was smart. Whatever attacked Andi, I almost hoped it would come after me. Of course, I had no idea what I would do if it did, but I wanted my chance to take a pound of flesh.

Besides, parking spaces were just as rare at night as they were during the daytime, so much so that they seemed to be on the endangered species list. Danger or no, at least by walking I didn't have to fight for a parking spot.

I heard the club before I saw it. A dark techno beat gave the place a spastic heartbeat that sounded almost sick. Andi called it "dubstep." I called it "anti-music" when she could hear me, "noise" when she couldn't. I missed the good old days of howling guitar solos and melodies and catchy riffs.

The little bastards could stay off my lawn, too. Damn, I felt old.

The club itself used a new type of business model in which two clubs, each with very different clientele, shared a building and operated under different names on different nights. On Mondays, Wednesdays, and Fridays, the club was "Elysium" and catered to the self-proclaimed "alt" lifestyle and featured neon, rave music, and only a vague laughable dress code. They weren't the ones that interested me. I wanted the Tuesday, Thursday, Saturday crowd, when the lights switched from bright neon to greens and reds, when the dress-code switched more toward crushed velvet, and when the hottest fashion accessories were a pair of custom fangs. Then, the club called itself "Nocturnity," and catered to people who fancied themselves vampires.

Not real vampires, of course. The fact of the matter was, most of Nocturnity's patrons were just normal people during the day who needed the outlet of a fantasy life at night. Wall to wall, the club's clientele included bank tellers and teachers, grocery baggers and managers, and any other wannabe whose life sucked just enough that the thought of being a soulless damned thing seemed like a good alternative. Most of them had no clue what real vampires were, and if they saw one, they would most likely fill their britches and sob.

I walked to the door and tried not to notice as the girl who took my cover charge gave me the once-over. Unlike everyone in the club, I didn't own a pair of tall boots, leather pants, or a frilly-sleeved shirt. In my usual garb of a bowling shirt, blue jeans and red high-top sneakers, I stuck out like someone's dad at a high-school kegger. I didn't have to put on the air of disinterest to look tragic and lonely. My personal history somehow etched itself deep in the scars on my face so even strangers knew my eyes had seen real tragedy. Also, the mummified arm helped. And I was in no mood to play games.

After a brief exchange with the doorman, I made my way to the back of the club where the owner du jour sat on, honest to Goddess, a throne, draped in a couple of nearly naked girls whose parents undoubtedly would question their daughters' life choices. From his gray slacks to his frilly-front shirt unbuttoned to the navel, the guy's demeanor screamed "douchebag."

"I'm looking for the owner," I shouted over the din.

"You've found him," he said. "I'm Shadow Ravenwood."

It took me a full beat to let the name sink in, and every ounce of self-control to keep from laughing in his face.

"I need to talk to you," I said. "In private."

He smiled and gave a dismissive wave. The two girls slid down off the throne and sauntered away, then Ravenwood stood and gestured for me to follow.

As we crossed the club, eyes stabbed at me through the darkness. I was used to stares and whispers, but not for being the most normal person in the room. I shifted my perception as we walked. The room went from a dank dungeon to a technicolor wash of rainbows. The energies surrounding the patrons were in almost every shade, every strength. Many had dots of brown, damaged psyches and broken souls. A few had flecks of red, rage and pain that bubbled beneath the surface, ready to lash out. But no one in the club seemed diseased or malignant. Even the owner, whatever his real name was, looked more like an insecure child with his energies laid bare. His girls were just apologies waiting to happen and a few daddy-issues short of a drug overdose.

But the one I looked for wasn't there. No one in attendance radiated black.

I switched my perception back and the club returned to industrial hell.

Ravenwood led me through a heavy door at the far end of the dance floor. As he pushed it closed, the heavy beat settled into a low pulse that didn't threaten to crack my skull open.

"What can we of the Vampire Court of Pittsburgh do for you, Mister Cooper?"

"You know me?"

"Why of course we do," he said with what I was sure was supposed to be a dramatic laugh. "Everyone in our community knows of your reputation and your abilities. We were devastated to hear of the passing of Miss Perry."

I bristled.

"But what brings you into Nocturnlty?"

"A friend of mine was in here two nights ago," I said. "Something in here got hold of her. Something bad."

"Surely you don't think one of our patrons..."

"She showed up on my doorstep suffering from severe blood loss and torn to shreds. Drink receipt in her pocket had the name of your place stamped on it."

What was left of the color drained out of his face.

"That's absurd," he said. "It couldn't have been anyone from here." He tried to make for the door, but I stepped in front of him. Under red lights, he looked like a Goth god, but under fluorescent tubes, I saw him for what he really was. Just another geek in a costume. He fancied himself as the romantic version of the vampire, with linen suits and Eurotrash accents, but he didn't know what a real vampire looked like. Odds were if he ever saw a real one, he'd turn into a blubbering coward and beg for mercy as it ate him. In his little kingdom, he could be king vamp, but in the cold light of the real world, he was just a little man playing make-believe.

"I don't think you understood," I said. "My friend got hurt in your club. I'm tired of my friends getting hurt. Am I making myself clear?"

"Yes," he stammered.

"What's your name?"

"Sh... Shadow..."

"Your real name?"

"Lawrence," he said, and as he did, all that remained of his courage deflated.

"You need to tell me what happened, and how my friend got hurt."

Lawrence turned out to be about as useful as an artificial

knee would be to a snake, and almost as fake. Once I managed to intimidate him, his whole character crumbled and he begged me not to sue.

Funny... I never used to consider myself intimidating. In fact, no one else ever did either. The world used to regard me as just another pudgy schlub with wild hair and bad fashion sense. But the scars on my face and the ruined arm seemed to have an effect on people that I didn't count on. I mean, I expected them to whisper and point, but a few looked at me as someone who'd seen some serious shit, and lived to tell the tale.

I exited the club and hoped my heart would return to its regular rhythm once removed from the overwhelming thump of dubstep. Carson Street stood almost quiet, unaffected by the goings on inside Nocturnity, and I breathed deep the first open breath since I went inside. Too many people, too much weird, too much negative energy.

On the sidewalk outside, local artists had set up card tables and easels to show off and sell their work. One sold chain mail jewelry while another sold beads and repurposed junk. A table sat littered with crude sculptures of little monsters, and an artist painted planets with only spraypaint and cardboard.

"You don't belong here, do you?"

I almost didn't hear the voice, it was so soft. The speaker sat on a stool beside an easel, charcoal in her hand. She didn't look at me as she spoke, but somehow there was no doubt as to whom she addressed.

"Excuse me?"

She smiled as she drew, her hand a graceful flourish of movement. Behind her rimless glasses, her eyes shone.

"For starters, I bet you're older than ninety percent of the yahoos who go in there," she said. "Second, you look lost."

Maybe I was.

I glanced up at her wares. The majority of her work was oil on canvas, but there were a few pieces in charcoal pinned up to a clothesline. The subject of each one was dark, but beautiful. The oil paintings captured the city in vivid color, but only one in particular caught my attention.

Heinz stadium. A moonless night. Green light that poured from a man suspended in sacrifice.

"Were you there?" The words caught in my throat like barbs.

She shook her head.

"I see things sometimes," she said. "Sometimes, what I see is pretty scary."

I knew the feeling.

She finished the drawing and frowned at it, then she gave me an appraising look.

"You don't belong here at all," she said. She handed me the

sketch. In it, I stood, withered arm and all, while something dark and sinister stood behind me. The black creature threatened to swallow me up, but the posture of my image gave the impression that I wouldn't back down.

"You keep that," she said. "Call it a gift to a good man."

"How do you know I'm a good man?"

"Like I said," she shrugged. "I see things sometimes. And more than a couple times, I saw you."

She walked the fine line between intriguing and creepy well, and it was all I could do not to stare. But old habits kicked in and I lowered the walls of my perception until the night street leapt into vivid technicolor. The building pulsed with the music, shades of pink and blue and gold. The other vendors glowed in shades of blue and green, all with little or large brown spots in their auras. But the girl shone bright in silver and blue. Streaks of brown highlighted her glow, but they gave way to swirls of starlight.

"Not sure what it is you're looking for," she said, "but it's impolite to stare."

"I'm sorry," I stammered. "I didn't mean to..."

"I'm Lily." She smiled and thrust out a charcoal-smudged hand. She caught me so off guard with her smile that I took her hand without regard for cleanliness.

"Stan."

"So why are you here?"

"A friend of mine got hurt here," I said. "I'm looking for what might've done it. Maybe I can stop it happening to someone else."

She glanced at the drawing.

"I see," she said.

"You haven't seen anything, have you? Like anything weird or out of the ordinary?"

She looked down at the pavement, then reached under her table and withdrew a sketchbook.

"I haven't seen anything," she said. "But... well, look."

I opened the cover and felt my blood turn to ice. In the images, the same dark figure that stood behind me loomed over fallen people, victims that lay helpless in black pools of graphite. As I flipped the pages, the dark presence got bigger, grew more intense in shape until I came to a page that made me stop cold. In the image, the shape tore and attacked a young girl. There was no mistaking the outfit, the hairstyle, the rings in her eyebrow.

"Andi."

Lily snatched the book back and jammed it into a rucksack, then set to work putting her paintings and sketches into a large portfolio.

"I can't help it," she said. "I see what I see. That was your friend?"

"Yeah."

"Is she..?"

"She's alive," I said.

Lily let out a breath.

"The others, I don't think they are," she said.

"Maybe you can help me."

She paused and stared long into my face with soft brown eyes that burrowed past my flesh and into my soul.

"You'll need all the help you can get," she said, her voice disjointed as if she weren't aware of why she even said it. "Here."

Lily took the picture out of my hands and scrawled something across the front, then she pulled on a bright pink coat.

"Now who looks like they don't belong," I said.

"More than you," she smiled as she shrugged her backpack onto her shoulders.

Behind her table, a hatchback waited for its mistress. It took her only a matter of seconds to pop the hatch and put her belongings in the car. How she managed to get an easel, a table, a stool, and the rest of her gear in I couldn't guess, but I stood transfixed as she smiled and slid into the driver's seat. The engine sputtered to life and she backed onto Carson Street, then headed toward the West End.

Whoever she was, she saw them, saw it, and I didn't want to lose her. If it figured out she saw, it might go after her, and I couldn't have her death on my conscience as well.

I glanced down at the sketch. The dark thing behind me oozed evil and malicious intent, and for a moment, I marveled that anyone could put so much malice onto a piece of paper with a stick of charcoal. Then I noticed the bottom of the page. She had signed it. Lily Fitch, with a great sweeping "L" and "F," with a phone number beneath.

I tucked the drawing under my ruined arm and headed back to the shop. Lily Fitch. I rolled the name over in my head and on my tongue.

5

The screen on my phone blinked as I debated pushing the button that would call Lily Fitch's phone number. I didn't know what to say, or even why I thought about calling her, but somehow my fingers punched her number in while my thumb debated joining their traitorous cabal. We'd only just met the night before, and only talked for five minutes, but it still seemed like cheating somehow. And how could I even think of another woman when Maggie was gone and Andi lay in intensive care? I let out a frustrated breath and flipped my phone closed, number undialed, as I exited the elevator in Mercy Hospital.

The stench of disinfectant burned my nostrils and turned my stomach as nurses paged doctors over the intercom. Their weird tinny voices did nothing to help my mental outlook. It seemed like the longer I stood in a hospital, the more my nerves frayed. It was little wonder. After all, my first hospital visit, I died and came back. My second was because of severe burns that came about because of some moldy South American rat demon. After that, I lost count or track of times or reasons, but there was never a happy story attached. My arm. My face. My best friend. Hell, I even chased a deranged necromancer into a hospital once, and wound up in jail for it.

A few months ago, the last time I had set foot inside Mercy Hospital, Maggie died. My son was born, but the only woman who ever truly, unconditionally, loved me had paid for it with her life. So, as I stood in the sterile beige and white room, my innards churned like a clutch of snakes.

Andi lay still in the bed, a tube in her arm and an oxygen mask strapped to her bruised and scratched face. A big gauze patch taped to her neck completed the image.

"No sign of sexual assault," said the doctor as she glanced at her records. "So at least there's that. This seems to be a case of simple assault."

"Have you called the police yet?"

"Of course we have," she said. "Any time there's a case of obvious assault, we're required by law to file a report."

"Good," I said. "When they show up, would you please keep me informed?"

The doctor nodded and left me alone with her.

Such a small girl, almost a waif, but there was so much more to Andi than hot pink hair streaks and knee-high stompy boots. So much power lay inside her that it was a wonder that something had actually gotten close enough to hurt her. Which, of course, begged the question: What could be so powerful that it could get to her?

But the figure in the hospital bed looked anything but imposing. Her skin had lost its usual pale glow for a more gray shade, and her sharp eyes stayed closed. I often forgot just how tiny she really was, but the figure in the bed was less the most powerful natural witch I knew, and more a young girl who fought for her life.

"Stanley." Barney materialized beside the bed. I was used to it.

"What's up?"

"I was just checking on her."

"You don't even know her. Why?"

"She's important to you," he said with a shrug. "Which makes her important to me."

"Thank you."

"I need you to know," he said. "What's inside her now? It can't get out to the rest of the hospital. And if it takes her over completely..."

"It won't," I snapped. "She's too strong."

"I hope you're right," said Barney. "As a precaution, I've set defenses around the room. She can't go out, and nothing bad can come in. Just until we know for sure."

"Until we know what for sure?"

"What's inside of her."

"Make sure the rest of the hospital is protected too," I said. "Whatever got her might come back and try to finish the job. I don't want anyone else to die."

Barney nodded, then faded into nothing.

I leaned close to Andi's ear.

"Gotta go," I whispered. "You're in good hands here. Fight. Don't you dare give up. I can't lose you, too."

Some say our lives are measured by the company we keep, or the impression we leave behind. I used to be of the opinion that our worlds were measured by the things we carry with us. Memories, love, that sort of thing. But it isn't true. I know now that our lives are measured, our worlds are measured, by the things we've lost. When a person loses something important, it creates a hole in that person's life. And that hole, that gaping wound, is the point around which he measures the things he still has. Put simply, we can't appreciate what we have until we've lost it, and then we fight like hell to get it back. Or we don't. We fight or we give up.

I lost Maggie. I was determined to fight like hell for Andi. Whatever got her, whatever infected her, had to be stopped. And

I was the only one around who seemed to be willing to do something as stupid as try to stop it.

That's me. Super Stan. Cue theme music.

I only had one real lead. The club was the scene of the crime. Whatever was going on happened there, or nearby. Which meant I needed to pay Nocturnity another visit. But as it was an off-day, I wound up in what appeared to be a completely different club.

Although it was only around two in the afternoon, the doors were open and employees hustled around to transform the place from Goth-hell into something decidedly fluffier.

As I stepped through the doors, a dozen eyes regarded me, then went back to their jobs.

"We're not open yet." The woman attached to the voice was taller than me by a good couple of inches and wore cut-off shorts and a tank top. A thick blonde braid hung down her shoulder to her waist, and a cigarette dangled from her ruby-red lips.

"Hi," I said as I tried to put on my least threatening face. "My name's Stanley Cooper. I was hoping I could maybe talk to the owner..."

"That's me," she said. "I'm Cassiopeia."

What was it with people and the fake, bullshit names? Tons of ancient societies used false names to avoid persecution or being caught, but in the modern age, such things just weren't necessary. The clown that ran Nocturnity went by something so ridiculous and cliché that it took all I had not to laugh in his face. For once, I wished I could run across someone in Pittsburgh that didn't have some sort of identity crisis.

"What's your real name?"

"Cassiopeia," she bristled. "My parents were hippies. Now, is there something I can do for you, or are you going to stand around pissing me off all day?"

Wish granted, and I felt like a royal jackass for it.

"Sorry," I said. "I didn't know... The other guy gave me some fake name..."

"Oh, him," she snorted. "Yeah, he has issues with reality. What can I do for you?"

I left out a few key elements, but I told her the gist of the story. Friend got hurt, I wanted to keep it from happening again. She seemed uninterested.

"What happens at that freakshow is not my problem," she said. "Bad enough I have to share a building with them."

"Have you noticed anything... weird?"

She glanced around the club.

"You're kidding, right? Weird is what we do. In fact, the weirdest thing I've seen in a while is you."

She was right. Whether it was a club for vampire wannabes or whatever crowd frequented Elysium, I didn't belong.

Cassiopeia turned to bark orders at someone. When she did, I noticed a few nasty scars on her back.

"Were you attacked too?"

She turned back to me and smiled.

"No, I did those. I'm into suspension. Those were from metal hooks through the meat of my back when I got hung about fifteen feet in the air."

I nodded like I knew what she meant, even though I didn't, and beat a hasty retreat for the door. The club was a dead end. Too much crap going on, too many people with damaged pscyches. What Andi saw in either place was a mystery to me.

As I stepped out into the sunshine, I pulled out the cell-phone that Maggie always insisted I keep.

I don't like cell phones. They creep me out. If I switch my vision, I can watch the energy move in and around peoples' heads, and I figure it can't be good for anyone. But I still keep it for emergencies.

I flipped it open. The number Lily Fitch gave me rang and rang, then I got a pre-recorded announcement that the user's voicemail was not set up.

"Dammit," I huffed as I slipped the phone back into my pocket and headed back down the street.

As I walked, I noticed that Carson Street seemed almost normal in comparison to the club. Sure, everyone had their quirks, and Cassiopeia seemed like every other merchant on the street, but the little vampire twerp was grade-A weird.

The chime on the shop door tinkled when I walked through. Every time I heard it, I expected Maggie to come through the curtain and kiss me. I expected Andi to look up from behind the counter and smile. Instead, the shop was empty, the lights dim. No customers. I suspected the shop wouldn't let anyone in.

"I'm working on it," I said. The walls shuddered.

The countertop was a long plank of natural ash, stained from years of oils from bottles and loving hands. A thousand transactions had worn the top smooth and provided a rustic look to the shop. There was no counting how many times she'd blessed something on the counter, held a patron's hand as they asked for advice. As I put my hand on the wood, I almost felt hers in mine.

The bell over the door tinkled. An older woman dressed in black peeked inside.

"Excuse me," she said. "I think I'm supposed to come here for help."

I blew out a deep breath. Life went on. No matter how much I wanted it to stop.

"What can I do for you?"

"I need..." She looked down at her shoes. "Oh, I feel silly asking. I need a clairvoyant."

For a moment, I wondered why, then I saw the shadow behind her. It flashed from a hazy outline to focus. From the glimpse I got, he was in his early twenties when he died, and the trauma on his neck was eerily similar to another wound I knew of.

"I can try to help," I said. "Come in."

In the old days, the handful of legitimate clairvoyants in the world were often lumped in with the charlatans, and nobody really knew how to separate the cream from the crap. People who claimed they could see ghosts popped their toes and lifted tables with their knees in dimly lit rooms to the delight of people who paid them for their services. It was quite an industry, until Harry Houdini decided enough was enough. He made it his personal mission to debunk all the hokum and bull, and the few legitimate psychics out there often hid from him in fear. Then the age of technology made things easier for hucksters like Bradu to impersonate legit psychics, but no matter what, people still wanted the old ways. People still expected darkened rooms and theatrics, even in the modern age.

The old woman, Doris, sat on one of Maggie's bar stools in the back of the shop, purse clutched tight to her chest.

"He disappeared a few weeks ago. The police haven't been able to find anything, but I'm sure he's dead."

"Why do you think that?"

"Because," she said. "I've felt his presence in the house since he disappeared. It feels like he's trying to contact me or something."

"Contact you how?"

"I'm not sure," she said. "A cold breeze. I saw a handprint on the foggy bathroom mirror yesterday. It's like he really wants to get my attention. Just yesterday, I heard the door to his room slam, and I was the only one in the house."

I glanced up at the shadow behind her.

"Yeah," I said. "I'd say he's trying to get your attention."

"Shouldn't we be sitting at a table? Maybe holding hands?"

"I don't need that," I said.

When I first developed my "gift," I couldn't turn it off. In fact, Maggie was the one who taught me how to build walls in my mind to keep myself from seeing a constant horror show of corpses and how they died. The tall shadow behind Doris stood silent and still behind her, vague and unassuming. Then I switched my vision.

The shop's pulse leapt into brilliant color, as did the life force of everything around me. And, sure enough, an angry twenty-something with a neck wound stood behind his mother, dressed head to toe in Goth-wear.

"Is he with us?" She looked around the room in a dramatic

fashion. I tried not to groan and roll my eyes.

"Yeah, he's here. What's his name?"

"Edward," she said.

"I prefer Balthazar Thorne," said the wraith.

I couldn't help but snicker.

"What do you need to know?"

"What happened to him?" said Doris. "He disappeared. I knew he was dead. I just knew it." Tears rolled down her cheeks.

"Aw, c'mon, Ma. Don't cry." Ed-thorne dropped the act for a moment and went to hug his mother. When his arms passed through her, she jumped a little.

"Was that him? Was that my Eddie?"

"Yes, ma'am," I said. "What do you want to ask him?"

"Can he hear me?"

I nodded.

"Eddie... What happened to you? Why didn't you come home? I waited up all night."

The ghost looked up at me, as if he expected me to repeat the question.

"You heard the woman," I said.

"I... I don't know," he said. "I was at this club, and I was leaving, and I walked out the door, and something hit me when I went around the building to get to my car."

"He was killed," I said. "I don't know how. Neither does he.

All he knows is that something hit him on the way out to his car, and his body was moved." It wasn't a lie. It just wasn't exactly the truth. No sense in upsetting the woman by telling her Ed-thorne was murdered by some supernatural beast. Better to let her draw her own conclusions.

"I knew it," she wailed as she sobbed into a handkerchief. "I knew no good would come from going to that bar."

"Let me guess," I said. "Nocturnity."

Ed-thorne nodded.

"Look... If you've got something to say to your mom, now's your chance to say it."

I expected a tearful goodbye. Maybe a disclosure of money stashed somewhere or at least a memorable sign-off.

"The weed's in my sock drawer," he said. "It's got a false bottom. It's all yours now. And Freddy is my dealer."

Unbelievable.

After a second of shock, I relayed the message. Doris seemed to brighten a bit, then rummaged in her purse.

"How much do I owe you?"

"Nothing," I said. "Not necessary."

"I insist," she said, then she crammed a wad of crumpled cash into my hand. Then she turned and scurried out the door. Ed-thorne made to follow her.

"Not so fast there," I said. "I need to ask you a couple of

questions."

The wraith lingered in the doorway.

"You need to tell me what you saw."

"Nothing," he said. "I saw dark and pavement, and that was it."

"Anything you can remember," I said. "I have a friend. She was attacked the same way."

"Is she..?"

"Alive," I said. "For now."

"I was walking to my car, then I heard this low growl, and something hit me from behind. Then it tore out my throat and left me on the ground. Then someone else came by and snapped my neck."

"Someone else? Like an accomplice?"

"More like a keeper. The thing that attacked me? Totally an animal."

"Anything else?"

"That friend of yours. Was she bit?"

"Yeah."

Ed-thorne shook his ethereal head and managed to look apologetic.

"Kill her," said the wraith. "She'll be better off."

Before I could form an appropriate reply, Ed-thorne wisped away like smoke.

When Maggie told me she was pregnant, I was terrified. My dad was my only fatherly role model, and I was afraid I could never live up to the old man's standards. Despite every assurance, I didn't think I was ready to be a dad.

The dirty diaper in my hand confirmed all my fears.

"What the hell have you been feeding him?"

Mother let out an exasperated huff as she brought over a clean diaper.

"Well, certainly not any of the hippy food you keep in this apartment," she said. "I went out and bought him formula."

Mom's "formula" seemed more like something one would get from Doctor Jekyll than Gerber, but I was too tired to argue. In the end, all that mattered was that his nutritional needs were met, and Daniel was a fat, happy baby.

I scooped him up and took him to the crib in my bedroom. As I laid him down, our eyes locked. It might've been my imagination, but something pushed at my mind, a force that pressed against the surface tension of my own mental bubble.

"What?"

Alien thoughts invaded my mind, simple, yet in such a barrage that I could scarcely keep up. Every one was a simple emotion. Hunger, cold, love, wonder. A baby's thoughts. Daniel's.

As fast as I detected them, I threw walls up to keep Daniel's thoughts out of mine. If I could sense his emotions, I was pretty sure he could feel mine, and no child needed to be privy to his parents' innermost thoughts. That sort of thing could scar a child for life. I couldn't even imagine the damage that could be done to Daniel if he were exposed to the level of uncertainty and sorrow that I felt. As soon as the connection was cut, Daniel cried.

"What's the matter?" Mom burst into the room ready to snuggle my son's tears away. As soon as she cleared the door, he stopped crying.

"How'd you do that?"

"Little dear knows his grandmother's voice," she said with a smug grin. More likely, he knew her thought patterns.

"He's just not used to me."

"Well, it's no wonder. You're always out at night doing God knows what. That's no way to be a parent."

"Go home, Mom."

She looked stunned.

"Go on. I can handle my son for one night."

Her face tightened around her anger.

"What about..?"

"*Mom*. Please. You need a break from Grandma duties. I appreciate all the help. I really do. But I've got to do this some-time, right? Go home. Get some rest. I'm not going anywhere tonight. I promise."

She still looked unsure, but her expression eased a little.

"If you're sure," she said. "I'll be back in the morning. If you need anything, you call."

"Yeah, yeah. I will. I promise."

Mom gave me an appraising look, then bent down to kiss Daniel on the forehead. Then she scooped up her purse and zip-zopped her way to the door. Before she left, she kissed her finger-tips and pressed them to the doorframe.

"Keep them safe," she said. It was a little unsettling, but gratifying to see her embrace something out of the ordinary about my life. The door closed behind her.

I lifted the blind to watch as my mom got into her car and pulled away. Only after her taillights cleared the parking lot did I let out a huge sigh of relief.

Impossible to spell "smother" without "mother."

Daniel was already sound asleep, so I pulled the door of the bedroom almost shut, then sat down on the couch. My butt hit the cushion and, as if by Magick, Bitsy the wondercat leaped into my lap.

"Where've you been hiding?" She regarded me closely with emerald eyes that made extended blinks as I stroked her head with my good hand. Bitsy wasn't my cat. She was Maggie's. And she missed her friend. I was a poor substitute, but I'd have to do. Maggie wasn't coming home.

Andi's laptop lay dormant on the coffee table, a mystical portal to all human knowledge, to which I didn't have the key. Computers dumbfounded me, and Andi's doubly so. Her "mod-it-till-it-breaks" philosophy of computer ownership left her with a piece of machinery that was more powerful than it should've been, and encrypted to the point of uselessness to anyone who didn't have the password. Like me. In Andi's hands, it was the greatest library in the world. In mine, it was a doorstop.

Everywhere I looked there were reminders of the two most important women in my life. One gone for good. One in a desperate fight for her life. For her soul, if Ed-thorne and Barney were to be believed. And I was useless.

A while ago, I had used the energies of my ruined arm to tap into Bitsy's emotional state. It gave me a sense of what the cat wanted, what she thought, and how much she despised such an invasion of her privacy. But more important to me, it gave me insight. Through force of will, I could create an arm, invisible to most people, that was strong, in place of my ruined flesh. I could use it to "possess" my own arm, give it mobility again, but it took supreme concentration. I didn't have Maggie to help me master the skill anymore, so it fell by the wayside.

But as I sat on the couch, I wondered what else I could do with a physical extension of metaphysical energy. I already knew I could read a cat. Maybe I could use it to read a computer.

I summoned all the will and intent I could muster, then shifted my sight and focused on the ruined arm. Energy poured out of my core and down the scarred appendage until the ghost arm formed. Then I stood over the coffee table and Andi's laptop. With a deep breath and momentary question of my own sanity, I slowly dipped my ghost arm through the laptop. The results were less than spectacular.

I didn't gain any knowledge, nor did I become the living embodiment of the entire internet. Instead, there was an audible pop and sizzle, and the light that indicated Andi's computer was in "sleep" mode went out. The distinct scent of burnt plastic and regret filled the air.

"Oh, shit!"

The spectral arm vanished along with my concentration and confidence and I used my good arm to pull the cover open. The screen stayed black.

"No," I said. "Don't do this. Please. C'mon..." I jabbed the power button five or six times. When the little light stayed dark, my hope sank. Not only was Andi in the hospital, I had just destroyed her laptop. She was going to kill me. I resolved to make up a lie if she recovered.

Not if. When.

I awoke to Bitsy gnawing on my foot. Several empty beer bottles on the coffee table sat in silent judgment of me, the man who slept on the couch instead of in his own bed because he feared the baby in his room. I rubbed my face and glanced at the clock. It was just before two in the morning.

"What?"

Bitsy sat on the end of the couch, ears back and tail puffed like a bottle brush. The pupils of her eyes were wide open, black holes ringed in emerald fire. She stared at the window and let out a low growl.

I crept to the window and peeked between the blinds.

The alley between the shop and the building next door was dark, poorly lit by a single overhead light. It was wide enough for a city garbage truck to get through, but only just. The dumpster sat in a recessed area surrounded by discarded cardboard and bags, courtesy of the neighbor.

A figure stood in the alleyway, hooded and covered in a long black cloak. At its side, on a chain, another figure crouched.

Where the first figure looked like a refugee from a costume shop, the second was almost naked, grotesque and gaunt. Its spine protruded from gray and yellow skin and red eyes glowed from within deep sockets. For a moment, I assumed it was the victim of possession, but then I shifted my vision.

What I saw stole away my breath and made me back away from the window.

The energies of the building reached out in a protective shield into the alleyway, as I expected. The cloaked figure stood bathed in swaths of red, brown, little wisps of green and purple, but no sign of demonic possession. I expected the other figure to radiate black, maybe with a thin corona of color, but what I saw left me confused and terrified.

It cast no aura. No blue, no black, no red. It was, for all intents and purposes, dead. So dead, in fact, that any residual energy was long dissipated. Yet it crouched in the alley, coiled, feral. Ready to strike and maul anyone who came near. It bore the vaguest resemblance to a man, but it was something far more insidious.

"It's okay," I said, and hoped Bitsy believed me more than I did. "We're safe in here. We're protected."

As if it heard me, the cloaked figure released the chain, and the beast snarled. It leaped for the stairwell, only to be knocked backward by the protective energies of the shop. It staggered a bit, then regained its footing. With a mad growl, the creature stalked toward the stairwell. When it reached the protective bubble, it pressed. Flesh smoked, but the red eyes only widened as it pushed further and climbed the stairs on all fours.

From my vantage point, the creature disappeared. I ran to the front door. Despite the strong urge, the need to know, the door stayed locked. But I stared out the peephole. I had to see how far it would get.

In the fish-eyed scape beyond my doorway, the distorted creature climbed the stairs, a spidery nightmare. Every step it took, the energies ripped at its body, tore more flesh, burned a bit more. The agony it must've felt had to have been unbearable, but it continued on until it got to the landing. It sniffed the air and glared at my door. Foam dripped from jagged teeth as it stood to its full emaciated height and stared at the peephole. I got the impression it could see me. Its long tongue lolled out of its mouth and licked the peephole, then it raised one clawed hand and scratched at the door, slow down the metal, high-pitched and terrifying. Bitsy hissed and darted into the bedroom.

The nightmarish creature snapped its head to the side, as if it heard some signal that I didn't, then it hurried down the steps on all fours.

I stood at the door long after it was gone, transfixed, as if welded to my spot by the horror of a thing that wasn't supposed to exist. But it did exist. And it was someone's pet.

Popular culture neutered the idea, put them in tuxedos or made them brooding pedophiles, called them the "lonely ones" or romanticized their existence until they became a groan-inducing joke. But the beast that climbed my stairs wasn't the kind of animal that seduced or pouted. It wasn't the type of creature that spoke in a vague European accent or even tried to blend in with normal people. The creature I saw was a huge serving of death, plain and simple, without airs or graces or anything that modern-day filmmakers gave. It was a perversion of life, the type of creature that would strip the flesh off a child's bones to sate its bloodlust and stalked its prey like a jungle cat. The claws I saw could probably cut through metal and the teeth would make short work of any body parts they came into contact with. The creature I saw was the real thing, about which old stories were written, and with which parents tried to frighten their children.

It was a vampire.

Not some fanciful asshat in a cape that pretended to drink blood as a metaphor for love; a real, terrifying, vampire.

And someone had it on a leash.

I stayed at the door until morning. Everything I ever knew about vampires came from books, from Maggie, from movies. I didn't know what was real and what was make-believe. But one thing everyone seemed to agree upon: The light of day could kill one. When the sun came up, I was fairly certain I was safe.

If it had wanted to get in, it could've. The shop's protection might've troubled it for a few minutes, but I had no illusions. It could've gotten in and ripped me to shreds. It could've hurt Daniel. The hooded figure wanted me to know. Wanted me to see that I wasn't safe.

Message received. Loud and clear.

When my mother's car pulled into the alley, I breathed a sigh of relief. Mom could be a pain in the ass, but she was also something else: A doting grandmother. And the perfect person to take Daniel out of town so he wouldn't get hurt.

It took me all of five minutes to convince Mom to take Daniel back to Washington with her. The chance to show off a new baby to her usual crowd of proud grandmas was too great to pass up. She packed his diaper bag, barely gave me a kiss on the cheek, and was gone before I could even say goodbye.

Funny, but I thought I'd be okay with his being gone. I thought it would be liberating to be relieved of diaper duty. But I missed him the moment Mom took him out the door. And I wanted nothing more than to hold him.

But there were things to do.

The shop had to remain closed for a while. The usual clientele knew what erratic hours we could keep, and a note on the door was sure to attract the wrong kind of attention. There was nothing to be done about it, though. No note, no explanation, the shop just had to be closed. I hoped she would understand. The door locked behind me as I went out to my car.

I didn't drive often. Maggie drove everywhere, partly because of the gimpy arm, but mostly because I just didn't like Pittsburgh traffic. But there were a few places too far to walk, and what I needed was interred in one of them.

The drive across town was uneventful, blessed by daylight and ignorance. Warm amber sunshine filtered through the car's windows, but it didn't stop the chill in my bones. It didn't keep my eyes off every dark alley I passed. And in each little urban cave, I imagined I saw red eyes, embers that waited to set the city ablaze in panic.

My apartment building felt like an old sweater. Maybe too small, maybe a bit smelly, but comfortable. I knew every hanging thread, every creaking board. I felt the comforting electricity of the protection wards I had woven into the sheetrock when the building was redone. Nothing evil could get past the threshold of the building.

But then, I thought that about the abomination too, and it made it to the door. I shivered at the thought.

My apartment was better protected than most. I'd had the wooden door changed out for a steel fire door years ago. But on

73

the back of it, runes and sigils ran its length and breadth. It made it the perfect place to hide.

And the perfect vault for things that didn't need to get out.

I fit the key in the lock and turned it, then pushed the door open. On the couch, a doll sat.

Case in point.

Its white sailor suit was still pressed and crisp while the little stuffed tiger in its hand still roared with adorably fearsome countenance. The thing wore a placid smile that could have been a smirk as easily as not. But the bottoms of its shoes were dirty, proof that the thing on the couch was no ordinary child's toy.

"What're you doing out?"

The damned thing tried every day to get out of its room, and every now and again, it succeeded. I closed the door behind me before it got any smart ideas and made a break for it.

"I don't have time to deal with you right now," I said. "I'm looking for something."

The spare bedroom was the vault, the place where I kept odds and ends that were too dangerous to be left out in the open. Artifacts, emblems, objects of power and books of forbidden knowledge, all tucked away in the heart of Steel City. It wasn't that I exactly liked having them around. I just didn't trust anyone else to keep them out of harm's way.

What I needed wasn't a cursed object or haunted gizmo.

It was a simple book, one that might've been found in any old bookstore, if any still existed. I found it a couple of years back in a mom-and-pop shop on Carson Street. The shop was gone, but the book was a real find.

I flipped through the pages until I found what I wanted.

Vampires. Blood-sucking, life-stealing vampires. The joke of the supernatural world to everyone except those who'd met one. They existed in one form or another in the myths and nightmares of every culture in history, and went by hundreds of names. Ungeheuer, strigoi, bantu, jikiniki... All names for the same type of creature. A walking corpse that fed off the blood and energies of the living.

According to the book, vampires kept their intelligence and used their long lives to amass power and to stay hidden. Most accounts made them out to be cunning, cruel even. But not feral. Not like the creature I saw in the alley. Which begged a question.

What could be so terrible that it could enslave a vampire and reduce it to a drooling hound?

I read through until I found passages about how to kill it. Most of the legends were either complete bullshit or worked on anything, whether vampire or not. The stake through the heart? Sure it would work, but then, a slab of wood through the heart would kill anyone. The same for beheading. I kept reading.

Many legends had it that they couldn't see their reflections in mirrors or that crosses repelled them. One even stated that all vampires were obsessive-compulsive and would stop to sort buttons if thrown at them. All bogus.

But the legend of daylight was accurate. The sun's rays could reduce a vampire to ash in a matter of seconds. But the ash had to be mixed with salt and washed into the ground to keep the creature from rising again.

I shut the book and put it back on the shelf.

As I turned to leave, I caught sight of my couch. My empty couch. The little bastard moved again. The last time I lost sight of it in an open room, it tried to slash my Achilles tendon. I scanned the room, hopeful that I wouldn't see it too late.

The doll sat on the kitchen counter, next to an open beer.

"Have one for me," I said. "I don't have time to mess with you today."

I turned the light off as I closed and locked the door.

I have a long and storied relationship with the fine officers of
the Pittsburgh police force. The majority of them seem to
think I belong either in jail or the nut house. Some of them feel
sorry for me. Some of them still blame me for the deaths of two
of their own, though they'd never say it to my face. But there are a
few who believe I play it straight with them, and that I'm usually
just in the wrong place at the wrong time.

"Leave me alone, Cooper." Detective Mark Menold stormed
out of the office he shared with three other detectives.

Case in point.

"C'mon," I said. "Can't you just look?"

"Not my case," he said. "Your friend's assault is being
looked into by one of these other clowns."

"Other people have been hurt," I said. "And at least one I'm
sure is dead. A kid named Edward Langille."

Menold stopped in mid-stride.

"His mother came to see me," I said. "How many have gone missing?"

I didn't have to see his face to know he was pulling the same look I pulled when Maggie had a valid point and I didn't want to hear it.

Used to pull.

"Goddamn it," he muttered as he turned to face me. "With me."

He led me down the hallway toward the interview rooms. They used to be called "interrogation rooms" until some time in the 1990's when someone felt "threatened" by the name and sued the city to have it changed. The decor was the same though.

Menold closed the door and motioned for me to sit in one of the uncomfortable chairs.

"Edward Langille, officially, is a missing person," he said, his voice low. "His mother declared him missing about a week ago."

"He's dead," I said. "Murdered by the same thing that put Andi in the hospital."

"How did you come by this information?"

I cocked an eyebrow at Menold and stared for effect. After a moment, he got the idea and rolled his eyes.

"You talked to him."

I nodded.

"Okay, so tell me something I can use. What killed him?"

For a moment, I ran through my explanation in my head. Even to myself, it seemed ridiculous. I could only imagine just how stupid it would sound to Menold. Any seasoned cop with his badge firmly pinned to reality would probably cuff me and order a psychiatric evaluation for even broaching the subject. But Menold and I had been through a lot together. He knew I didn't bullshit.

"It was a feral vampire that's being controlled by someone at Nocturnity."

A good three seconds passed before he blinked.

"Bullshit," he said.

"It came to my apartment last night."

He stood without another word and marched to the door, then opened it and stared at me.

"I'm not making it up."

"Out."

"Mark..."

"Out!"

I got up and made for the door.

"Detective Norman is looking after Andi's case. Go talk to him. And if you value your freedom and what little reputation you have around here, you won't say anything about any fucking vampires. Got me?"

I nodded. He wasn't to blame. Not really. The weird world I lived in cost him two cops he respected. Things most folks were taught were nothing more than legend and superstition were real in my world, and his rules didn't often apply.

He shut the door behind me and walked the opposite way down the hall.

Detective Norman, I found out, was more eager to meet me than I was to meet him. As I came through the door of his office, he almost leapt out of his chair to shake my hand.

"Detective Shannon Norman," he said with a vigorous pump. "Or Shannon. Or Detective. Whatever. It's so good to meet you, sir."

"Um... Why's that?"

"I've been following the case files that you've assisted on. It's a real honor to meet you."

On the inside I cringed. Hard. I hoped it didn't show.

"Can I get you something? Coffee? Soda?"

"Where are you at with Andi's case?"

"Of course," he said as he regained his composure, if not his dignity. "Well, when she wakes up, we'll get an artist down there, try to get a description of who attacked her. She wasn't raped, so that's a plus, right? Basically, we're just waiting on her."

"What about under her nails? The attending physician said there was skin under her nails."

"Yeah," said Norman. "About that. We collected all the samples and sent them to the lab. The guys in the lab said they never got them. Said the baggies we sent over had nothing in them but dust, if you can believe that."

"Damn it..."

"Do you have any information we can use?"

"She was at this club on Carson called Nocturnity when she was attacked. It's a vampire-wannabe place..."

"I know the club," he said with a grin. "I've been there a few times."

My cringe must've shown through.

"Oh, don't worry," he said. "I'm not one of those weirdos. I've been there on busts. Lots of party drugs there."

His expression shifted.

"Not that I think your friend is on drugs," he stammered. "Or a weirdo. It's just... well, we get reports and..."

"It's fine," I said. "Could you just keep me informed, please?"

"Absolutely," he said. "Can I ask you a question?"

"Sure."

He rested his chin on his fist.

"What's it like to see dead people?"

The question hit me hard with its blunt edge. The look on his face told me he wasn't making fun of me, but the childish enthusiasm that flashed through his eyes was more than a little frightening.

"It sucks," I said as I exited.

There are a great many places that are pretty much always haunted, in my experience. Old homes, theaters, even airports lend themselves to paranormal activity. All supposedly-haunted places have a common thread, and that's high levels of emotion. Love, hate, fear, ecstasy: all emotions that cause a human body to put off more energy, and that energy leaves scars or imprints. People hear the word "haunted" and assume a violent death was involved, but that's not always the case. I can't count the number of places I've been that were "haunted" by nothing more than memories of a really good sex life.

The number-one spot on the ranking of haunted places belonged to the undisputed champions of emotional extremes, hospitals, which was another reason I tended to avoid them. Shifting my vision inside one threw me into a panorama of horror shows that I could never forget. But, for once, the hospital was the number one place I wanted to be because I wanted to be there when Andi woke up. The apartment over the shop came in second, in case someone needed to find me, or on the off chance that exhaustion would claim my body and I could rest.

I stood in front of the third place on the list, almost afraid to enter. Nocturnity pulsed again against the natural heartbeat of Pittsburgh. There wasn't much I could do there, but it felt better than sitting on my ass and waiting for something else to happen. To guess by the quality of clientele that entered the club, the level of emotional scarring on Nocturnity would be very high.

"This place, huh?"

Detective Norman stuck out worse than I did. His grey suit with the dark blue tie screamed "cop," while his cheerful smile and over-friendly attitude let the world know he didn't have a whole lot of experience.

"Andi was here when she got attacked," I said. "The drink receipt in her pocket puts her here right before she showed up on my doorstep. Whatever got to her, I'm betting it's in there."

"Good bit of detective work," said Norman with a shrug. "Let's go say hello."

Almost like someone flipped a switch, his demeanor went from soft to hardened. The goofy smile was replaced with a straight-line mouth and eyes that seemed able to cut glass. The gentle droop of his shoulders straightened into a wide authoritative stance. As he went through the door, the lovable clown was gone, replaced by a no-nonsense cop in a bad mood.

The door-person caught the scent of Norman's attitude,

and picked up the house phone before the door even shut behind us. She spoke quickly, eyes darting between him and me. When she hung up, she put on her best I-wasn't-doing-anything smile.

"Welcome to Nocturnity," she said. "How can I..?"

"Skip it," said Norman in a voice harder than I thought him capable. He flashed his badge. "I'm investigating an assault that happened in your parking lot. Word has it there have been more than a few others disappeared or hurt here in a similar fashion. Care to comment?"

The color drained from her face.

"The owner will be right down, officer..."

"*Detective* Norman," he said. "Mind if we look around while we wait?"

He didn't wait for an answer, but walked straight through the curtain to the main club. I followed quickly and nodded to the woman without so much as a smile.

Inside, the Shannon Norman I knew returned for a brief appearance.

"Is this cool, or what?" The dopey grin sat just as easy on his face as the hard line did. "So, like, can you do your stuff and see what we're looking for?"

On the inside, I cringed. Truth be told, I was going to "do my stuff" anyway, but to hear him say it made the whole process uncomfortable. But he was right. I needed to See.

When I'd switched my perception before, I didn't know what I was looking for. I figured I was looking for some run-of-the-mill bad guy, maybe someone who got his jollies off beating up and robbing girls. I didn't think there might be something more malevolent involved.

The darkened club leapt into vivid color when I opened my eyes. Just like before, every color of aura in the spectrum was represented. And, just like before, I didn't see anything or anyone that radiated evil. I did, however, see things I didn't notice on my first visit.

Amid all the crushed velvet and plastic fangs, more than a dozen faces stared at us. Each victim's face had the same lost expression. Each of them pleaded with their eyes. Dead, all of them. Their images retained the bloody damage left on their bodies by the horrific attacks. I studied their faces and made a silent promise to each of them that I would help in some way, then I switched my vision back because I couldn't handle the way they looked at me.

"Do you see anything?" Detective Norman scanned the crowd.

"Not what we're looking for."

"Mister Cooper!" Shadow Ravenwood gushed in grand fashion as he approached, as if we were old friends. "How good to see you again. And you are?"

"Detective Shannon Norman," he said as he flashed his badge. "I'd like to ask you a few questions about your club."

"Yes, of course," said Ravenwood. "Any friend of Mister Cooper's is a friend of Nocturnity and the Vampire Court."

Norman stepped to close the distance between them with frightening speed.

"Get this straight. We're not friends, and I don't give a shit about your club. I'm investigating an assault, and I'm just looking for an excuse to shut your little freakshow down."

"Of... Of course," he said. "I'm happy to cooperate."

"Stan, why don't you hang out here? Maybe you can see something I can't."

Detective Norman gestured for Ravenwood to take him to the office, which left me alone in someplace I was sure came straight from Dante's nightmares. Not for the first time, I wished Maggie were with me.

Before I could order a drink, or even figure out how to order one, the flesh on my back crept up around my shoulder blades. Every hair on my neck prickled, and what was left of the tattoo on my ruined arm stung. My heart rate jumped as my mouth went dry. Something stared, watched me from a distance, but close enough that its eyes bored into me like drill bits. I had to get outside, put some distance between me and whatever it was. I needed air.

I cleared the door at almost a dead run. The cool night air tasted good as I gulped it into my lungs, but my heart still pounded. Whatever was in there, it was bad enough to turn my insides to jelly and my knees to wet noodles.

People gawked and whispered as they passed by. A few snickered about what drug they thought I was on, but I didn't care. I just had to be away from whatever was watching me.

"I didn't expect to see you around here so soon."

Lily Fitch, sketchbook in hand, stood in front of me on the sidewalk. The light hit her glasses to obscure her eyes behind rectangles of white.

"Geez... Are you okay?" She stuck out her hand to help me up. "You don't look so hot."

I raised a hand to signal her to give me a moment while my lungs decided whether or not to keep working. She put an arm around me and guided me away from the club and toward a bench on the sidewalk. I sat before my legs gave out.

"I'm fine," I lied. "Just got a little woozy."

"Bullshit," she said as she flipped open her sketchbook. The page she opened it to was rough, crude even. But even so, it was unmistakable. Me, on the floor, while a dark shape stared down. "I hoped this was one of the false visions, but I guess not."

"On the nose," I said. My head cleared and my heart rate slowed to normal. "I need to go back in. I left..."

"There you are!" Norman hurried up the sidewalk, a big broad smile on his face. "Thought you left me hanging. You okay? See anything?"

"Plenty," I said. "Just not what I was looking for."

"And you are..?" The smile left as he stuck his hand out to Lily.

"Lily," she said. Norman gave me a sideways glance.

"She's a friend," I said.

It struck me as odd that I called her a friend, even though I'd only met her once before. But something about her demeanor, about the way she spoke, told me she was someone to be trusted, and someone I wanted in my life.

"Detective Norman," he said. "Nice to meet you. If you'll excuse us."

"She already knows," I said. "She's seen it. Just... What did you find out?"

Norman gave an exasperated look to Lily, then the eager smile returned to his face.

"The owner of this place is a real tool."

No kidding.

"No way he had anything to do with anything."

I hated to admit it, but I agreed. When I stole a look at him earlier, his aura had lots of colors in it, but nothing to indicate evil. Like it or not, I had to admit I'd reached a...

"Dead end."

The midnight clientele of Eat-N-Park is, for the most part, the same as it is at any other twenty-four-hour restaurant. The faces range from exhausted to manic, angry to joyful to horny, too sleepy to be out or too wide awake not to be on something.

Norman sat on the side of the table between Lily and myself. He held his coffee, but his eyes darted between us like he was certain one of us was going to make some sort of move. Lily chewed on a fried mozzarella stick and drank her chocolate milkshake while I stared at my basket of French fries and the little bowl of gravy and wondered why I'd ordered it. After the night I'd had, I wasn't really hungry.

"So how do you two know each other?" Norman dumped a packet of sweetener into his mug and gave it a slow stir.

"Just met," said Lily between bites. "We bumped into each other outside the club a couple of days ago."

"Nocturnity?" Norman stopped stirring, considered, then continued.

"I went to see what I could find out," I said. "Lily had a stand outside."

"And?"

"And nothing," I said as I picked up a limp fry and examined it. Cold. "She sees things and draws them. She offered to try to help."

"Uh-huh." Norman took a drink of his coffee, made a face, and dumped another packet into the mug.

"I really do," she said. "See things, I mean. And I want to help."

"Ma'am," said Norman. "I can appreciate that, but I don't know you, and I don't know anything about you."

"So what do you want to know?"

"I want to know what makes you," he pointed at me, "trust you." He pointed at Lily.

Her eyes dropped down to her basket of cheese sticks for a moment.

"I'm sorry," she said as she pushed her chair away from the table. "I just wanted to help. I didn't mean..."

"Whoa," I said. "Please, sit down. Detective Norman is just being cautious. Show him the drawing you showed me."

Her eyes met mine, questioning, then darted to Norman, then back to me.

"Why should I?" Her focus shifted back to her cheese sticks. "He won't believe me. No one ever does."

"I do," I said. "Give him a chance."

"My sketchbook is in my car," she said. She got up and headed for the door, but she left her purse on the table. When she was out of earshot, I turned on Norman.

"What the hell, man?"

"What? I shouldn't be skeptical? Come on, I'm a cop. It comes with the territory."

"Okay," I said. "But you believe me. You trust me, right?"

"Absolutely."

"Then give her the benefit of the doubt, okay?"

I knew what it was like to have no one believe. I knew what it was like to have people whisper behind my back and call me names like crackpot and huckster. I also knew how good it felt to have even one person in a room full of skeptics believe. I didn't want Lily to have as hard a time as I had.

"Okay," said Shannon, hands raised. "I'll ease up, but this had better be some drawing."

The bell over the door chimed as Lily came back inside, sketchbook under her arm. The look on her face showed her hurt, but also the determination of not letting Norman get the best of her. When she arrived at the table, she opened the book and handed it over.

Norman stared at it for a moment, brows furrowed, then his eyes went wide. He looked from the sketch to me, then back to Lily, then back to the sketch.

"Okay," he said. "I'm convinced."

"Just like that?" Lily's concern cracked and fell away.

"Yeah," said Norman. "Just like that."

"Why?" I was overjoyed, but still wanted to know.

"You weren't there, were you?"

"No," she said. "But I saw it in my vision. Why?"

Norman placed a finger on the picture of my attempted martyr. "You see that?"

I leaned over the table. His finger was under a single face, one person in a sea of humanity that was in the stands that night. The face was unmistakable.

"That's me," he said.

We said our goodbyes soon after that. Norman was kind enough to pick up the check for everyone's food, and Lily seemed overjoyed to have someone else who actually believed in her besides just me. She shook Norman's hand, then leaned in and hugged me. For a moment, I forgot where I was, and just enjoyed the warmth of her body, the softness of her hair on my face.

"Thank you," she whispered in my ear. Then she kissed my cheek, got into her car, and drove away.

Norman gave me a wry smile.

"She's cute."

"Knock it off," I said.

The entire ride home, he didn't say anything, but he sat there with a stupidly smug grin on his face, like the bastard knew something I didn't.

8

A long time ago, I learned that a lot of what some people call fate and others call divine planning is little more than happenstance. The streets people walk down, the cities they live in, the neighborhoods where they grew up, all determined by random factors that could easily have gone the other way. A right turn instead of left, a catch instead of a miss, and everyone might be living very different lives. My mother, for example, liked to tell me that my "incident," as she called it, was a curse that put me on a dangerous path. But if I'd used a different harness, or even called in sick on the one specific day that mattered, it would never have happened. And, if it weren't for that one seemingly random incident, I would never have met Maggie. I would never have met Taylor, or watched him die. Or watched Maggie die. I wouldn't have ever burned my arm up, or fought to save the world, or a thousand other things.

And sometimes, I wished I'd called in sick.

But for every bad thing that happened to me, a thousand good things resulted. I found Maggie and, consequently, the first real love of my life. I met Andi, got to live in a bizarre living building, and I got to help people. And I had a son.

Not to mention that whole saving-the-city-and-world-and-existence thing.

And since helping people was what I did best, I figured the best way to occupy myself the next morning was to try to lend a hand at the Pittsburgh police station. Of course, not everyone shared my viewpoint.

"Why are you here?" Detective Menold glanced up from a folder full of photos. "I thought you and Detective Norman were out clubbing or something."

"How many missing persons cases are you working on right now?"

"None of your business," he said.

"Can I see the photos?"

"No."

"Why?"

He looked up from the stack with an exasperated huff.

"Because, regardless of what I do or don't believe, most people in this office think you're a nut."

"Do you?"

"I said it doesn't matter what I believe." He looked back

down at the folder.

"Do you?" I leaned closer until he dropped the photos in his hand as looked back up at me.

"No," he said. "I know you're legit. Taylor knew it, and so did Appel. But they're dead and I don't want to wind up that way myself, understand?"

"But I can help you," I said. "You know I can. Just let me see the pictures."

Appel shook his head and shoved the folder my way.

"Fine," he said. "Be my guest. But I can't exactly act on any leads just because you say so. I need evidence."

"Yeah," I said. "I know."

I sat down and flipped through the folder. The fronts were diverse: school photos, family holiday pictures, modeling shots. The backs told names, last-seen dates, and other information the police needed. Of the more than two hundred photos in the file, I recognized about a dozen of them. Those got set aside while I finished my perusal.

"These," I said when I handed them back to Menold. "These people are dead."

"How do you know?"

"I saw them. At Nocturnity."

"Which means what?" He crossed his arms and leaned back in his chair. "No evidence that they died there. No evidence of what killed them. Only that you say they died there, and there's no proof."

"What kind of proof do you need?"

"Bodies would be nice," he said. He dropped his arms and shook his head. "Look, man. I know you want to help, but I can't use any of this just on your word. There's due process, evidence, investigative procedure... All little rules I have to follow. I can't just close the folders on these cases."

"I know," I said. "I just thought maybe you'd like a point in the right direction."

"And I appreciate it," he said. "I do. But I have to do things the right way. Now go. Visit your friend in the hospital. If I find out anything, I'll have Norman get in touch with you, okay?"

I didn't answer, but turned and left. Of course he needed proof. Taylor took me at my word, but Menold always looked at me with an eye toward skepticism. It didn't matter how much I wanted to help, the police needed to work within the confines of due process. And I did too, unless I wanted to be arrested.

The street outside the station hustled in the morning light. Cars zipped for a few seconds before traffic ground them to a stop, pedestrians passed the frustrated drivers, and, in general, Pittsburgh woke up with the same agonized cough as it always did. The same way a person would if he didn't get much sleep the night before. Or the night before that one, either.

My head pounded. It occurred to me that I needed coffee in the worst possible way.

"Hey!" said a familiar voice. "Wait up!"

Detective Shannon Norman hurried down the front steps.

"Where're you going?"

"Coffee," I said.

"I'll join you."

Perfect.

There was, once upon a time, a bitter elixir brewed from the grounds of a humble coffee bean that got the world running on schedule and powered empires with its mighty caffeinated jolt. Simple in its formula, the supplicant bowed at the base of the almighty percolator and begged the gods for just a taste of the hot brown beverage to kick his soul into high gear, and to provide him with the necessary energy to start his day. All one needed was a pot, coffee grounds, and water.

Those days are long gone.

Norman and I stood at the counter of Caribou Coffee and goggled at the menu. Amid all the fancy, television-inspired names, I couldn't find the one thing I craved, the base of all things lovely in the world of jittery caffeine, a simple cup of coffee. But, to me, a good mocha was an acceptable substitute. We placed our orders and sat down at a table.

"He didn't believe you, did he?"

"I don't know," I said. "I want to think he did, but evidence and all..."

"That sucks," said Shannon. It seemed weird to think of him as "Detective Norman" in a coffee shop while we talked like friends. "If it helps, I believe you."

"Why?"

His eyes dropped as he fidgeted with his napkin.

"You know that drawing Lily showed me? I believe you because I was there," he said. "Heinz field. About a year ago. I saw what happened. Look, I was one of the cops that thought you were crazy before. But I was wrong. I saw what you did, and I'm thankful. As far as I'm concerned, you're the closest thing to an honest-to-God superhero I know."

"I don't know what to say."

"Yeah," he said. "Well, there's more. I've been seeing some weird shit going down lately. I notice things that just don't seem right, and I don't have explanations for any of it."

"Like what?"

"This thing with your friend," he said. "I requested this case because I recognized what the hospital report said about her injuries, and about where she was."

"You've seen it before?"

"A couple of times. We found one maybe about a block

from the club in a parking lot. The other we found in a field, but they both looked like they'd been mauled. What caught my attention were the torn areas around major arteries. And that the bodies had significant blood loss that couldn't be accounted for. Of course, the other bodies had broken necks."

The barista called our numbers and Shannon got up and claimed our cups. As he sat back down, I couldn't help but shift my perception. I needed to know. If he was full of shit, his aura couldn't hide it. If he was on the level, he was the ally I needed.

"Go ahead," he said.

"What?"

"You're doing that thing you do, right? Where you see my energy or whatever? Go ahead. I've got nothing to hide from you."

Busted.

Still, the invitation stood. I shifted my perception, lowered the walls in my mind and let the real world flood in. When I opened my eyes, the man in front of me looked very different. I expected to see browns, blues, other hues that told me his life story. But what I saw gave me pause. The colors were there, yes. But beneath them all great swaths of red and brown the colors of rage and despair, churned and bubbled. Shannon was damaged, emotionally beaten down and pretty pissed off about it, but the layers of cool blue and green always overrode the anger. He was a good man. An honest man. But a man for whom rage was an issue, and very different from the smiling person I assumed sat in front of me.

"Anger issues?" I took a sip of my mocha as I replaced the walls and closed the doors.

"Yeah," He said. "There's actually more to it than that, but yeah, that's what it boils down to."

"Want to talk about it?"

"Some other time," he said. "You look dead on your feet. Didn't you sleep last night?"

I'd tried, but I just couldn't. The beast at my doorstep still gave me the creeps, for one thing. For another, I missed Daniel. And then there was that kiss that still felt warm on my cheek where Lily had placed it. I doubted I'd slept more than thirty minutes, if that.

"Not really," I said. "Too much on my mind."

"Go home," said Norman. "Get some rest. Check on Andi. When I find something out, I'll call you, okay?"

"But..."

"Stan, you're no good to anyone if you're too tired to function. Go get some sleep."

I wanted to argue, but then again, the thought of a few hours of shut-eye sounded really good. I agreed and headed home. The coffee was too good to waste, but I was too tired for it to stop me from a nap.

There was a time when I dreaded sleep. Every time I closed my eyes, all the most horrific events of my life played out in graphic detail. My death? Check. The time a couple of crazy people tried to sacrifice me to bring about the end of the world? Yep. But my nightmares had stopped a while back because of Maggie. After a while, I stopped being afraid of sleep, and even looked forward to the velvet black embrace of naptime. Then Maggie died, and with her, the spell she'd woven to keep the nightmares at bay. They seemed determined to make up for lost time.

Still, my body could only take so much. I closed my eyes and hoped for a peaceful slumber.

"Cooper!" The voice was accompanied by thunderous raps on my door, the kind that only belonged to one person. "Cooper! You awake?"

I dragged myself out of bed and staggered to the door. As I figured, Menold stood on the other side. Norman stood next to him, head down, hands clasped in front in the fig-leaf position.

"What?"

"Can I come in?" Something wasn't right. Menold's demeanor was off and Norman looked bereaved.

"Sure," I said. "What, you decide you need my help after all?"

"You'd better sit down," he said.

I did as he asked.

"There was an accident," he said. "We found your mother's car off Highway 79. It was rolled."

My stomach knotted as I tried to digest what he meant.

"Your mom's alive," blurted Norman. "But she's in critical condition. We found a baby's car seat. Did she have..?"

"My son," I said. "She was taking my son to Washington to be safe."

"We didn't find him," said Menold. "Just your mother."

"What do you mean, you didn't find him? Is he alive?"

I had pushed Daniel off on my mom, not only so he would be safe, but because I didn't know how to handle a kid. I'd wanted him out of sight, out of mind. But all I wanted at that moment was to see him, and he wouldn't be out of my mind again. Ever. My hands shook as guilt washed over me. My kid. My responsibility. My fault.

"We don't know."

"But he was in the car with her! When was the wreck?"

"We don't know yet," said Norman. "We're trying to piece it together. Looks like a tire blew out and she ran off the road and flipped her car."

"But my son! Where's Daniel?"

"Stan," he said. "Listen. We're looking for him. We're going to find him. I promise."

Menold stood up to leave.

"If there's anything I can do to help you," he said. "Officially or not. You call me. Okay?"

"Yeah," I said. "Sure. Where is she?"

"Mercy."

I got up, pulled on my shoes and followed them down the stairs toward my car.

"I've got to see her," I said.

"Look, Stan, I've got to warn you. The wreck was pretty bad. She's pretty torn up."

"I don't care," I said as I climbed into my car, started the engine, and backed out.

My mom's room looked just like Andi's. Same colors, same bed, same uncomfortable chair in the corner.

I hated that chair. It wasn't designed to help or heal. It was left so people would have a place to worry. It was a hard cushion, a big leather thing that gave the false impression of comfort, just like it gave the false impression of hope. I had spent too much time in such a chair at Maggie's side. I had spent more time in the one just like it in Andi's room.

And as I sat in the one next to my mother, I couldn't help but feel a little abandoned.

Menold wasn't lying about her condition. The gauze that covered her face concealed a gash that went across her forehead and down her cheek almost to her mouth. She wasn't able to breathe on her own, and she had more tubes in her than I cared to count. All I saw was another of the most important women in my life slipping away, and nothing I could do about it.

"Mom?" The only answer was the sound of the ventilator that kept her lungs active. "What happened? Where's Daniel?"

"You ain't going to get answers that way." Barney faded into existence at the edge of the room. "And you know it."

"She can't leave me too," I said.

"Son, if you want answers, you're going to have to ask the right questions. And you'd better be quick. She doesn't have much longer."

Despite the tears that rolled down my cheeks, I took a deep breath and centered my will, then pushed energy into my dead arm. After a moment, the lifeless appendage twitched and a pale blue arm, one made of my own life force, appeared. I reached with it until I was almost at my mother's face.

"It's not going to be pretty in there," said Barney.

"Let me do this," I said. My voice quivered with rage and regret. Barney faded away.

Before I could tell myself not to, I pushed my will into my mother's head and fell into her mind. Like animated portraits on the wall of a stairwell, scenes played out as I tumbled past. Some were beautiful, others not so much. My fall slowed, then stopped when I reached what I recognized to be as an exaggerated version of the apartment over the shop.

And there I stood. At least, my mother's image of me, full of rage. The ruin of my arm spread over more of my body in a grotesque exaggeration.

"You were a shit mother!" the other me spat. "I wish I'd died rather than endured what you did to me! Every mistake I ever made is your fault!" I'd never said it, but she heard it in every angry word I'd ever said. I was ashamed.

The scene shifted and ebbed until I sat in the passenger seat of her car, headed down Highway 376. In the back seat, little Daniel babbled and kicked his feet. Mom smiled up at him in the rearview mirror. She never saw what hit her, so neither did I. One moment, she puttered happily down the road, her dream of grandmotherhood fulfilled. Then sparks, screams, the squeal of twisted metal, and the din of collision. The car rolled. Mom reached for the back seat, her eyes locked on Daniel, then the roof caved in and she was crushed. Her hand flopped useless until the car came to rest.

I lay in the car beside her, unable to move, unable to breathe, unable to do anything but sob as my mother's breath grew more and more shallow. Then I heard footsteps in the grass.

Heavy steps.

The door to the back seat tore away, and hands reached in and unfastened Daniel's carrier. There wasn't a scratch on him, not so much as a hair out of place. The hands pulled him through the gaping wound in the car, and then were gone.

The car around us faded, and I stood in a blank void next to my mother.

"I'm so sorry," she said. "I didn't know."

"Mom." I tried not to choke on my own tears. "Can you tell me what happened? Where's Daniel?"

"They took him," she said.

"Who?"

"I don't know. But they said something funny before they left. I don't know what it meant."

"What was it?"

"Evergreen will rise again."

Even in my astral form, my guts turned to icy nails. It wasn't possible. Evergreen was disbanded. For all intents and purposes, dead. The psychotic leaders were turned to ash. The rest of the members were either dead or off trying to forget their association. Or so I'd thought.

"Are you sure that's what they said?"

"Yes," she said. "Oh, Stanley, I'm so sorry I have to leave you like this."

"You'll get better," I said. "You have to. I need you."

"I'm afraid not, pumpkin. I think I can already feel my body letting go."

"I'm so sorry I got you into this," I sobbed. "I don't want to lose you too."

"You'll never lose me." Mom reached out and caressed my face. "I'll always be with you in your heart. But I don't know what to do now. Do I just hang around?"

As much as I wanted her to stay, the thought of my mother as a ghost was more than I could stand.

"Maggie," I said. "If you can hear me, I need you now."

"You'll never lose me either."

Hers was the sweetest voice in the world, the only thing that could soothe me on a bad day, the only voice I'd wanted to hear since the day I met her and since the day she died. It wrapped around the back of my head like a warm soft scarf and pulled all the longing from me that I'd kept bottled up for months. Inside my mother's mind, I fell to my knees and wept.

"Stan," Maggie said. "I'm here."

I couldn't look. I couldn't bear the thought of seeing her again for the last time. What if she looked like she did when she died? Emaciated? Skeletal? It was the last image of her in my head already. I didn't want to see it again.

"I've missed you," I sobbed.

"I couldn't stay. Daniel took too much of my energy to stay earthbound. Where I am, it's... beautiful."

"Take my mother," I said. "Please. I don't care what it's called or where it is, but keep her safe."

She dragged her fingers over my ethereal shoulders as she walked past. The scent of vanilla and rosemary trailed behind her.

"There is an afterlife," she said. "And it's more than you can imagine."

I wished I could believe her.

As she passed, I opened my eyes.

Maggie. Beautiful red hair, full figure and all, stood next to my mother with a smile on her face. She wore a long white gown and had flowers in her hair. Her eyes sparkled just like they did when she was alive, and her smile was just as warm. She was the way I wanted to remember her, and my heart broke.

"I love you, Stan," she said. "I'll always love you. You've got to find Daniel. He needs you. And so does Andi."

"I can't do this without you."

"Sure you can," she smiled. "I believe in you."

Maggie and my mother faded, and I fell to the cold floor of the hospital room. Nurses rushed in to try to resuscitate my mother, but it was too late. She was gone. I sat on the floor and cried.

S ome say musicians are poets for the working class, and, as such, have the unique ability to tap into the human condition that people call emotions. Not the standard bubblegum pop garbage, but real musicians. The so-called "grunge" musicians have the ability to express angst better than anyone. Hair-bands from the 1980s can make person feel like life is a high school kegger. But blues artists like B.B. King and Junior Wells have a direct pipeline into a person's soul and have the ability to make wallowing in depression seem like a natural, almost acceptable thing to do.

Junior's Chicago-style harmonica wailed in the cold dark of the apartment, a mournful howl I would've made if I knew how to give my soul a voice. Two of the most important people in my life were dead, both taken far too soon. With Maggie, I had time to prepare, to think. But Mom was just... gone. No chance to apologize for being a rotten son, no opportunity to tell her how much she actually meant to me. Just gone.

Andi still lay in the hospital, and no one could figure out just what the hell was wrong with her. Barney seemed to know more than he let on, but all I could get out of him were riddles and non-answers.

And, of course, Daniel was missing. And I didn't have the slightest idea of where to look for him, or even how.

As low points went, rock bottom was a step up from where I sat.

Bitsy leapt into my lap and pushed her head under my hand.

"Not now," I said, as I pushed her off onto the couch.

She climbed back into my lap and pushed under my hand again.

"Get off me," I growled, and shoved her off again.

She climbed back into my lap.

"I said get off me!" I went to push her again, but she dug her claws into my leg and bit my hand. As I recoiled in shock, she stared up at me, her emerald eyes bored into my skull.

Bitsy was not an ordinary cat by any measure. Graceful beyond her form, strong despite her size. She was a creature of deceptive intelligence. Once upon a time, I'd sunk my phantom arm into her head and found out just how smart she really was, and I'd never really looked at her the same since.

She stared at me, and in my mind I heard the voice I just always associated with her.

Quit feeling sorry for yourself, it said. *Get up off your ass and go find your cub.*

It was the kick in the butt I needed. Maggie had left our son in my care, and so far, I was a piss-poor father. Andi needed me to find answers, and while my mom's style of parenting left a lot to be desired, my father didn't raise me to be a quitter.

I gave Bitsy a scratch on the head and reached for my phone.

"Are you sure you want to do this?"

Shannon Norman's car was tiny, cramped, and almost cartoonish, but at least he kept it clean. It didn't matter how big or small it was, though. I needed to be free to concentrate, not worried about where I was or what was around me. I once tried to drive with my vision shifted. A half-dozen near-accidents later, I resolved to never do it again.

"Yeah," I said. "Where is it?"

"The tape should be up still," he said. "We should spot it pretty soon. You sure you don't want to wait for daylight?"

"No time," I said. "Can't wait."

We got onto Highway 79. During the day, the road was a constant thrum of traffic. However, in the dark, we were only greeted by sporadic headlights, both in front and behind, as if everyone who passed knew something bad had happened, and were worried it might happen to them next.

Norman drove until we saw yellow tape. The car was gone, but the side of the road lay gashed open like a wound where it dug in. Broken glass lay off the side of the road, along with tiny pieces of debris that hadn't been collected by the wrecker. It was a miracle she'd lived as long as she had. Even more of one that Daniel was still alive.

We got out of the car and walked toward the tape.

"You're sure?" Norman looked uneasy. "I mean, once you see this, you can't un-see it, you know? You sure you want to see it?"

I didn't want to watch my mom's car roll over. Of course I didn't. I didn't want to watch someone take my son and run off with him, either. But at the same time, I did. I needed to. I needed to know who it was, and also why.

"Just stay behind me," I said.

My stomach fluttered as I closed my eyes and willed the doors and walls in my mind to open and fall. With every door that swung wide, every wall that lowered, another filter on reality came away until all I saw was the world without a lens. It was raw and terrible, beautiful and frightening at once.

My mother's car sped beside me and jolted as something

I couldn't see slammed into the side. Mom's face contorted in terror and confusion as her car listed over to one side, then sailed past on its top. My instinct was to run, to try to pull open doors that were no longer there, to try to save my mother and my son, but I stood still as stone and watched to see what would happen next.

Tires crunched gravel, and another vehicle pulled up. But I couldn't see it. I had an idea of a vague general outline, but in truth it was just a large black blur of smoke and shadow. As I watched, another blur stepped away from it and walked to the car. The back door bent and twisted as the blur pried it open, then my son floated out of the car, borne aloft by arms of shadow, and into the car-shaped blur. Then it returned to my mother's car, leaned down to the driver's smashed window and spoke to my mother. Then it joined with the car-shaped shadow and was gone.

"Nothing," I said as I replaced the filters on the world. "God damn it, there's nothing here."

"You couldn't get a good look at them? Their car? Anything?"

"No! Whoever it was, I couldn't see them. They just took Daniel and left!"

"How does that work?"

"They knew," I said. "They knew I'd come looking, and

they knew how to hide themselves from me."

"How would they know how to do that?"

"I don't know!"

"Well, at least there's one little piece of good news," said Norman.

I goggled at him.

"What? What the hell are you talking about? They took my son!"

"Yes," said Norman, calmer than I could've been. "And that's good news."

"How?"

"Because it means he's alive."

He was right. They wouldn't have taken a dead kid, would they? They ran her off the road to get to him, but how did they know that doing so wouldn't have killed him too? If they wanted him, it only made sense they'd want him unharmed. But wrecking my mom's car seemed to indicate the opposite.

"But we still don't know who or where they took him," I said.

Norman looked about to reply but was interrupted by his phone.

"Hello?" His forehead wrinkled and he frowned as his shoulders tightened. "I'm with him now. Yeah. We're on our way."

He ended the call and stuffed his phone in his pocket.

"Your friend Andi is out of the hospital," said Norman as he hurried back to his car.

"They discharged her?"

"She attacked a nurse and escaped," he said. "We need to go."

The hospital room looked like a crime scene, which it was. Blood splattered the floor and walls while the bed, far heavier than those most folk have in their homes, lay tipped on its side in a corner. The blinds lay on the floor, torn to pieces, below a broken window.

Officer Menold spoke to Norman just out of earshot, though they both glanced at me with alarming frequency.

"I don't know what happened," said Barney. "She was just laying there in bed, practically comatose, then she just sat up and attacked the nurse. Looked like she was trying to eat her."

"You know more than you're telling," I whispered. "What is going on with her?"

"Steer clear of her, Stan. If you see her, you'd do well by your own safety to run the other way. You should've killed her when you had the chance."

For a moment, I forgot I was the only one who could hear Barney.

"What the hell are you talking about? She's just a kid!"

"A kid who caused serious property damage and then committed assault," said Menold as Barney disappeared. "The nurse has lacerations all over her face from that kid's nails, and says she tried to bite her."

It couldn't be. It just couldn't.

"Did she get bit?"

"No," said Menold. "She managed to get away before that, then your friend jumped out the window."

"We're five stories up," I said.

"Yeah," said Menold. "I know."

I backed out of the room and into the hallway where the hospital continued its life, business as usual. Orderlies who cleaned up the blood didn't even look twice at it. Nurses attended the sick and dying with clinical detachment and continued their rounds. It didn't matter to them that what had happened in Andi's room had the potential to affect their jobs in the most profound possible way. Or maybe they just didn't realize how serious the situation was.

My phone buzzed in my pocket. I pulled it out and read the caller ID. The nurses didn't seem to notice as I ducked down the hall, away from the police, then pressed the green button.

"Andi?" I whispered. "Where are you?"

"I'm so scared," she sobbed into the phone. "I came home but no one was there. What's happening to me? Where are you?

Stan... Please... Help me."

"Just wait there," I said. "I'm on my way."

The good side about grief is it gives people an out. For the griever, it's the easiest thing in the world to say "I don't feel like it" or "I need to go home," and people respect it and leave him alone. For everyone else, a grieving person who wants to leave is a blessing because, while they want to help and be there, dealing with a grief-stricken person is taxing.

So when I told Detective Norman that I needed to go home, he didn't think twice about it. He didn't see me answer the phone, and I didn't exactly lie to him. I did want to go home. I just didn't tell him why.

Is a lie of omission just as bad as every other lie?

I waited until Norman's taillights disappeared around the corner before I turned toward the shop. My first instinct was to head up the stairs to the apartment, but I noticed the front door stood open, with tiny streaks of red on the wood. I took a deep breath and stepped inside.

The shop was bitter cold, the air stagnant, as if she held her breath in fear. It stood to reason. Andi was her "mother." How else would a child react when mommy leaves in an ambulance and comes home a...

"Andi?" My voice sounded strange, flat and muted in the

darkness. "You here?"

No answer. The hair on my good arm prickled and the spot where the protective tattoo used to be on my ruined arm burned. Every sound amplified as fear crept up my legs and across my spine.

I made my way toward the back room and paused at the curtain. She was inside. I felt her like a cold pulse, like ants under my skin. Every instinct I had screamed at me to run away, to slam the door behind me and never look back. But I couldn't. It was Andi. No matter what else she was, first and foremost, she was still Andi.

I pushed the curtain aside.

The room was darker than I thought possible. It had no windows, so it got plenty dark often. But the darkness beyond the curtain seemed almost solid, alive.

"Andi?"

In the inky blackness, two pinpricks of light appeared. Whether it was a trick of my mind, or if her eyes really glowed, I couldn't say. It did, however, scare the ever-loving hell out of me.

"Stan?" The pinpricks moved closer.

"Yeah," I said. "It's me." The urge to run was strong.

"Thank the Goddess," she said. The darkness thinned, and behind it Andi became visible. She still wore the hospital gown, smeared with blood and torn from the glass. In the corner, where

I'd seen her eyes, a small pile of dead rats lay. Blood smeared her mouth and hands.

"I'm scared," she said. "I don't know what's happening to me. And I'm so... hungry."

Her face turned from the sweet girl that I knew to some feral beast, mouth open, fingers outstretched toward me as she lunged. In that instant, the ice-blue eyes I knew held kindness were gone, replaced with obsidian orbs that reflected my terror.

But I knew just what to do.

"Holy shit!" I backpedaled as fast as I could through the curtain into the main shop. The walls around me trembled as Andi stalked her prey. "Andi! It's me! Andi, come on! Stop this!"

She snarled and lunged again. I dodged and managed to keep just out of reach, but I felt the wind as her outstretched fingers passed a whisker from my face. It wasn't her. Maybe the body still belonged to her, but the will was no longer Andrea Bedford. The hunger had hold of her, and there wasn't much to be done about it. At least, not in the front of the shop.

I maneuvered around until the door to the workroom was to my back. In the darkness, she let out a low snarl that promised nightmares for a month. It built in pitch and intensity until she sprang. I took the moment and ducked.

Andi sailed over my head and into the workroom again, but closer to my target. In the center of the workroom, a pentacle lay etched into the floor. It was Maggie's summoning circle, her place of power. I grabbed a mop with my good arm and threw all my will into the dead one. The bright blue spirit arm sprang forth, up like a shield.

She snarled again, then leaped toward me. I raised the spirit arm. When she struck it, she fell backward onto the floor. The flesh where I touched her smoked. As she screamed in pain, I pushed her with the mop toward the circle. It wasn't easy, but after a few moments, I managed to get her fully inside, then I slammed my hand down on the metal.

Most people can't see the effects of pure will in the world. They might see the results of such workings, but the real Magick is lost on them because they are trained, often from birth, to just not see things, taught to ignore the wondrous.

I, on the other hand, couldn't ignore it, and watched as the air around her hardened into a transparent shell composed of my energy and say-so. The walls around me shook in protest.

"It's for her own good," I shouted to the building. "She keeps this up, she's going to hurt someone! You want that?"

The walls quieted.

Andi clawed and screamed at the invisible barrier. It gave me a moment to get a good look at her. Grey, almost alabaster skin and wild onyx eyes made her seem much more imposing than the little girl I knew. I just hoped there was something left of her inside.

"Knock it off!" I shouted.

She seemed surprised for a moment, confused even, then her face returned to rage.

"C'mon," I said. "Can't even break a simple containment spell? What's the matter with you?"

Okay, to be fair, I had a plan. Granted, it was a terrible plan, and I had no idea if it would work, but it was worth a try, and Andi was worth the risk.

Her temper swelled, and as it did, the old memories in her head took over. She murmured as she drew energy into herself from every available source, then she threw her arms wide as the energy rushed through her core and out her extremities. The dome shattered. If I was wrong, I was in deep trouble.

As the energy shot through her body, recognition crossed her face. Her eyes returned to blue and her knees went weak and she dropped to the floor.

"Stan?"

"Hi."

"How'd I get here?" She tugged at the hospital gown before she realized she was naked beneath it. "What the hell is going on?"

10

It took me a little more than an hour to explain the basics to Andi, up to and including why she woke up to find herself attempting to eat me. It took slightly longer for her to accept it. Every little movement from her made me twitchy.

"I can't be." Tears rolled down her cheeks. "There's no such thing."

"Tell that to the one who came up and sniffed the door," I said. "They're real enough, and it looks like you've been infected."

"But I don't want to be a vampire!"

I couldn't blame the kid. Her life was hard enough without needing a fresh supply of human bean-juice to sustain her. We didn't even know what was pure fantasy and what was fact. All we knew for sure was there was a monster inside of her, it wanted to take control, and it was damned tough.

There was a knock at the apartment door. I knew by the way the thuds landed who it was.

"Got it," said Norman as I opened the door. He stood with a confused look on his face and a cooler in his hand. "Now can you please tell me why?"

I stood aside and let him see into the apartment, where Andi managed to look both afraid and terrifying.

"God damn it." He quickly shut the door as he handed me the cooler. "You know people are looking for her. She's wanted for questioning!"

"I know," I said. "But she's the only family I've got left right now, and she needs me. And I might need her too."

Norman nodded, but his eyes never left her.

Inside the cooler, four or five units of whole blood waited to save someone's life. I took one out and handed it to Andi. As if on instinct, she bit into the plastic and shuddered as she drank. Little drops of crimson fell from her lips onto the kitchen floor, but she didn't stop until the bag was flat and empty.

"Damn," said Norman.

We both stared until she was finished. I didn't want to, but I couldn't help it. She was, at the same time, so fascinating and so damned scary, I just couldn't help but watch.

As she finished, she noticed.

"Oh gods," she said. "That's disgusting... But..."

"Yeah," I said. "It's okay."

"Did the nurse..?"

"She's okay," said Norman. "And she's not filing a report. She said you looked disoriented, so she figures you weren't quite yourself."

"Yeah," she muttered. "I'm sorry. I could see myself doing it, but I couldn't stop."

"I figured," I said. "But what pisses me off is that Barney knew."

"Barney?" Norman looked confused.

"Ghost at the hospital," I said. "Long story. But he kept dropping hints and wouldn't just tell me."

"So maybe he knows something about my condition," said Andi.

"Later," I said. "I've got bigger problems now. Someone took my son, and I need to find him."

"Wait, someone took Daniel?" Whether it was her own protective nature or the newfound power that surged through her, her short-cropped hair stood straight out like quills. Finally, the expression "hackles up" made sense.

"Wrecked my mom's car to get to him."

"Your mom... Is she..?"

Oh, yeah. That's right. She didn't know.

"Dead," I said. "Whoever took him murdered her to get to him. Just left her to die in pain."

All her rancor deflated as she sat down.

"Goddess, Stan. I'm so sorry. I didn't know..."

"We're looking for leads," said Norman. "Tracking the site, but there's not much to go on."

"Go back to the station," I said. "Do cop-stuff. If you turn up anything, you'll let me know, right?"

Norman's brow wrinkled.

"What about you?"

"What else can I do?" I shrugged. "I have people to contact to tell them my mom died, a funeral to plan... You just don't let her killer get away clean."

Norman's shoulder's slumped as he nodded. The big clown was in a position I knew all too well, which was one of loss. He wanted to help, but he didn't know how, and the police force wasn't going to be much help either.

"I'll keep you informed," he said as he went out the door. "You do the same, okay? Let me know if you need anything."

I nodded and closed the door behind him. When his heavy footsteps left the stairwell, I turned back to Andi.

"I need you," I said. "I don't like going places alone, and you're still the most powerful witch I know. Can I count on you?"

"Of course," she stammered. "What do you..?"

"Get your jacket," I said. "It's going to be a long night."

Evergreen.

There was a time that I considered them my friends. Allies. A group of ever-changing numbers, but always the same core seven members. They met in a humble Monroeville bookstore to discuss matters metaphysical, religious ideals, and other things that made people think of them as just a bunch of hippies that were a little kooky. I was never sure how else to describe them.

But one went rogue, then another died, then two more decided they were best qualified to be gods of some new world order, and the whole group had just disintegrated in a flash of fire and screams.

I thought they were gone. I should've known better.

With most of the core group dead, I figured the best place to look for answers was with the surviving members. That meant my first stop was the tiny borough of Pitcairn.

The town itself had died a long time ago, but it was just too stubborn to admit it. There were more taped windows and boarded doors on Main Street than open storefronts. The only two businesses that seemed to thrive in Pitcairn were booze and religion. Every corner, it seemed, had a bar. And across the street sat a church for atonement for the sins earned on a barstool. And even they were dying out.

The church I wanted was off the main street, a few blocks in, older than the rest. The last time I had visited, the church's power and influence had radiated through the streets.

"That's weird," I said as I pulled up.

"What?" Andi was nervous, and rightfully so. If the folklore about her condition was true, the church grounds had the ability to fry her on contact, reduce her to ash without even time to scream. I didn't want her to go in, but to stay on the edge of the church's influence to act as a lookout. But as I pulled up, it seemed like it didn't matter.

"No power. It's almost like the building is..."

It wasn't possible.

"Stay here," I said as I threw the car into park and hurried across the churchyard.

The last time, the church's defenses were strong enough to knock me on my backside. Of course that had something to do with a demon that had taken up residence inside me at the time. When I'd tried to walk in, the old building had protected itself, and I'd wound up with a cracked tailbone for it.

Every place people go has an energy to it. Whether it's a home or a shopping mall, if people go there, they leave a bit of residual energy behind. With churches, where people whip themselves into a religious fervor, the energy signature is much higher and gives the building a life of its own. Old churches can be powerful buildings. Monsters, if left without a guardian.

The church should've been a real beast. Her energies should've been enough to repel any type of perceived attack. But it was cold. The palpable hum of life was quiet.

"No way." I shifted my vision. What I Saw brought tears to my eyes and made my stomach lurch.

Where gold auras and swirling energies had been stood cold black stone. No life, no colors, not even the corruption of energies to evil. What stood before me was an empty battery, a cold husk of a building. The church was dead.

"Is it supposed to look like that?"

Andi stood behind me. I was too stunned about the church to be startled.

"No," I said. It took me a full beat to register what she said. I turned and stared at her.

"Is this how the world looks to you?" She looked up at the top spire, then at the neighboring buildings. "I mean, you've told me about the energies and stuff, but I'd never seen it before. It's... It's beautiful."

"Yeah," I said. "C'mon."

The building should've deflected Andi. It should've knocked her backward and done everything in its power to keep her out. But the back door hung open on a broken hinge, and the air around it offered no resistance at all. Andi stepped through without so much as a whisper.

"Bob? You around?"

The church was home to one of Evergreen's more powerful

members, a man I only knew as Neighbor Bob. Whose neighbor he was, I didn't know, but he was devout in his belief system, and when the church fell into distress, it was Bob who kept it alive. More, he melded with it, became a living extension of it. If the church was dead, I had serious fears as to Bob's safety.

Every creak and groan echoed through the cavernous building, split along hallways and rebounded back into the great sanctuary. The oppressive darkness didn't bother me, really, so much as it gave me the feeling of damp hands on my neck. I wanted to shake it off and wipe the darkness away, even though every instinct I had screamed at me to turn around and run for my life.

"I shouldn't be in here," said Andi. "I shouldn't even be able to be here."

"I know," I said. "Just be ready to make with the fireworks if we have to get out of here."

The hallway stretched long before us. It was a trick of the light, a deep shadow that played on our most primal fears. Even so, every step I took felt like I was mired in glue. When we got to the end of the hall, neither of us wanted to open the door.

"Bob?" In my head I called it out. However, In the real world, it most likely came out as a pathetic whisper in the dark. "You in there?"

I held my breath as the door swung open. All I could see

was more black. It didn't matter. If Bob was in the building, the main sanctuary was where he would be. I took a few tentative steps inside. Even with my vision shifted, there was nothing to see. No radiating lines of power, no life force, no will. Just black. Just a hole where a church should've been.

"Andi," I hissed. "I need some light in here. Think you could..?"

Without another word, blue light erupted from a stone in Andi's hand. In my shifted vision, I understood.

"The dark's eating the light," I said.

"How?" Andi's voice had a far-away quality that I didn't like.

"I don't know," I said as I turned in place. "I've never seen... Jesus!"

I'd found Bob. The old man's body hung upside down, nailed in a crucifix pose, with his head toward the floor. His skin was taut against his bones, so tight it looked as if it would rip through. He looked more like an Egyptian mummy than a man I'd spoken to less than nine months ago. Whoever hung him on the wall had sucked all his energies, all his life, out of him. On the wall over his feet, in blood, someone had painted a familiar symbol. A pine tree in a circle.

"Evergreen," I said.

The light flickered.

"Stan," said Andi. "We need to go."

"In a minute," I said.

"NOW."

I turned to see Andi glassy-eyed as her jaw slack.

"I'm getting hungry again."

Shit.

Rule one of Magick: The laws of physics apply.

In the case of most spell-slinging, Einstein's notion that energy can neither be destroyed nor created holds true. It can only change form. Which means, in layman's terms, the more energy a person throws out, the more that person has to take in. Since Magick is, at its core, energy manipulation, all that energy has to come from somewhere. Someone like me, with a bit more fat on him that I'd like to admit, can go for a long while without refueling. Andi, on the other hand, weighed in at a buck-ten at best, and had no such stores of energy. For most of us, a giant sandwich from Primanti Bros. will serve to refuel for a couple of hours.

But Andi didn't eat normal food anymore.

Or maybe she did. How the hell would I know? I was just as new at the whole "vampire" thing as she was.

All I knew was she was hungry, and between me and the front door of the building, which put me in a very precarious position.

"Just hold on," I said. "There's another blood pack in the car."

Her body shuddered as the light in her hand dimmed. More energy out. And yet, I wasn't crazy about the notion of the two of us in pitch darkness together. Especially not when she felt peckish. Still, I reasoned, if she ran out of power before we got to the car, I'd still be in the dark with her, and she'd then be more hungry and try to eat me.

"Douse the light," I said.

"But..."

"Do it," I said. "Conserve your energy. We need to get to the car."

The light winked out, and to be honest, I was thankful. I couldn't stand to look at Bob's desiccated corpse any longer. If it was the same guy who killed my mother, there wouldn't be any more clues to be gained at the scene anyway. The big bloody tree on the wall was enough. Let the cops see if they could find anything.

As we reached the door to the sanctuary, a loud bang echoed through the building. Followed by another. And another. The sound of something like a pipe hitting walls. Someone else was in the church. If it was our mystery person, I wanted a word with him. If it was some random punk with nothing better to do,

I felt very sorry for him.

"I got this," said Andi. Her voice sounded strange, almost feral, like it did in the shop when she'd tried to eat me. Before I could say anything to stop her, she was gone.

"Dammit."

Andi didn't have enough experience to control her new-found hunger, and if the intruder was the mystery Evergreen member, I needed to get to him first. Andi would tear him apart before I got any answers, and Daniel might well be lost. If I could figure out where he was, I could protect him. Not that it was high on my list of things I wanted to do, but I needed to.

On the other hand, if it was just some random kid, I had to protect him from Andi. The last thing she needed was guilt heaped on top of her already overtaxed soul. If an innocent died at her hands, she wouldn't recover.

Either way, I had to play race-the-vampire.

I stretched out with my energies and flooded the hallways. What came back was a kind of psychic sonar image. Wherever a solid object stood, I perceived a barrier. When it moved, I "felt" it. It took me all of two seconds to find our intruder, and a half second more to locate Andi as she closed in on him.

He was big. Details didn't come through, but he was a lot bigger than me and probably weighed more than me and Andi combined. In one hand, he held what appeared to be a three-foot section of pipe. In the other, something roughly the shape of a whiskey bottle.

Vagrant. Dammit.

Andi didn't know the layout of the building like I did. He was closer to me than her, but I still didn't have much time. I hit the hallway at a dead run and trusted my sonar trick to guide me. It almost worked, too. A few bruises on the shins, a couple of places where I tripped on loose carpet, but it worked. I rounded a corner to see the big bruiser ready to swing the pipe, and Andi ready to drop down on him from above.

She hung like a spider, black eyes hungry, as she positioned herself over him. Poor bastard didn't even know she was there.

"Hey!" I shouted. They both turned to look at me. And I had no plan beyond getting their attention.

"What?" The guy was young, maybe in his midtwenties. He was also drunk out of his mind and had such a look of despair that I didn't need to see his aura to know he wasn't evil. Great swaths of brown and red flitted through his energy signature. The kid was disillusioned, in pain, royally pissed off, but not evil. He was also in the wrong place at the wrong time.

I dove for him as Andi dropped. It was only by dumb luck that she missed us both, but she hit the ground hissing like an angry cat.

"'Da fuck?" The big guy just sat on his butt and stared,

too wasted or too stupid to understand his life was in danger. I slapped him across the face with my good hand while I raised the energy in my phantom arm.

"Run, dumbass!"

He kicked his feet and scrambled down the hall and out the door. Mission accomplished, the big dumb goon was safe. Which meant Andi's sights were on me. Again.

"This is getting old fast," I growled.

She jumped at me, and by some miracle, I managed to get my phantom arm between us. The pure blue energy beat her back, knocked her sideways, but it didn't do much for slowing her down. If anything, she looked more angry than before.

"Just calm down." I tried to make my voice as soothing as possible, given the circumstance. It was like trying to talk down an angry Doberman. "There's food in the car. You want that?"

Then a thought occurred to me. A stupid, suicidal plan of a thought.

She lunged at me again, but instead of throwing her off, I met her head-on. Her strength was incredible. She was so tiny, yet she was stronger than a man twice her size. I said a silent prayer to Maggie for help, then jammed my ethereal arm into Andi's head.

The sensation was what I imagined it felt like to be turned inside out.

In my mind's eye, Andi's light grew dim. Behind her, a vile creature made of disease and malice, oil and sludge, pulsed and drained more of her life. The vampire, the creature that infected her soul, was a parasite. A demon, to be sure, but a parasite nonetheless. So many strings led from it to her that there would never be a way to cut them all. Every time one broke five more took its place. The vampiric part of her nature drained her until it was all that was left, and to keep it at bay, she had to feed.

Andi on a normal day had more energy than any other human being I knew. But she was weak, depleted from her time in the hospital, weakened by the creature inside her. There was only one thing left to do to keep it in check, loath as I was to do it.

"Take mine," I said.

Inside a person's mind, intangibles become reality. Most abstract concepts that are hard to grasp become physical manifestations. A person could say "ball" in the physical world, but in her mind, a ball appears, the object instead of the concept. Likewise, if a person talks about his body's energy, it manifests itself in a way that he can see.

My center glowed, and blue light flowed out of me like a river torrent. It hit Andi like a wave, and in the physical world, her body convulsed with the transfusion. I gave her as much as I could before I became too weak to fight, then I pulled back.

We sat in darkness. Through broken windows, moonlight

glinted off tears on Andi's cheeks.

"I'm so sorry, Stan," she said. "So sorry."

"It's fine," I lied. "We need to get out of here before you burn through what I gave you."

"Then what? You can't trust me anymore."

I lifted her chin with my finger and stared into her eyes.

"I trust you with my life," I said. "I trust you with my son. Maggie trusted you, and I will always trust you. We'll sort this out somehow. But I need you. Don't you dare quit on me. I can't lose you too."

Andi nodded and put her arms around my neck. I tried not to flinch. If I did, she either didn't notice or ignored it. Either way, she hugged me and cried on my shoulder while I tried to figure out my next move.

Bob was dead. The church was dead. There were only a few members of the Evergreen core left that I knew. One was close by. And she scared the hell out of me.

11

People often wear masks. From our day-to-day lives to what we do behind closed doors, people can often be completely different from what anyone else knows. No one would ever think that the mild-mannered data-systems employee dressed up like a zombie in a tux at night and put on a weird little public access program that showed public domain movies. People look at the cardigan-wearing librarian and are shocked when they discover her after-hours leather fetish. No matter who we talk to, it can be argued that we don't really know them, no matter how hard we try, because most people have at least two distinct personalities: public and private.

Andi wore a mask, though it wasn't one she wanted. In public, she kept up the image of an average twentysomething with tattoos and multicolored hair and everyday real problems. Behind the mask, a killer wanted to get out, to rip and tear and feast on the life force of anyone who walked past.

I had my masks too. I walked around like someone who was determined, strong and able to handle whatever garbage got thrown his way. Behind the mask, all I wanted was to sit in a corner and cry for my mother, for my lover, for my child. I was running on autopilot, and while I knew I wasn't really fooling anyone, it felt good to have busy work to keep me going.

Some people I thought were my friends had worn masks. To my face, they had smiled and laughed and wanted nothing but the best for me. When it came down to it, though, they'd really wanted to use me as a catalyst to bring about the end of the world. It had given me extreme trust issues, and my circle of trust got really small as a consequence.

Sunrise rumbled over the horizon, and Andi and I found out that at least one of the old legends about vampires were true. Sunlight. When the first rays touched her arm, a large welt formed and bubbled on the skin, then split and smoked. Andi dove into the back seat and huddled under a coat until I could get her back to the shop. Once inside, she hid in a dark corner of the workroom like a cornered animal until I calmed her down.

There was no way she was going out during the daylight, and even though I was exhausted, I couldn't rest. I decided to head out on my own and trust whatever power kept saving my life that I could survive until I found my son. I left the remaining blood packs in the workroom mini fridge before I left and made a mental note that we needed a more permanent solution.

An old pair of sunglasses in the center console of the car made the sunlight almost bearable, but the headache that throbbed with every bump in the road didn't let up. My body needed sleep, but my mind didn't dare. Too many unanswered questions, too many problems. Was there a way to help Andi? Who was left in Evergreen? And where was my son?

Daniel.

Again, I was reminded of what a piss-poor father I was. The first sign of trouble, I sent him away. And if I hadn't, maybe they wouldn't have gotten to him. Maybe my mom would still be alive. Or maybe they would've come for him anyway, and I'd be dead with no hope of rescuing him.

I pulled up into the quiet suburb and parked across the street from a small, unassuming, average-looking house with a white picket fence and a manicured yard. It might just as well have looked like Dracula's castle to me. The place creeped me out to no end. And its owner was one of the most terrifying people I knew.

And her husband had no idea.

Reneau wore masks better than anyone else in the world. In the daytime, in public, she was the perfect image of a house-wife. But those of us who saw her away from the PTA and frilly apron knew her to be a formidable woman, one with Magick to spare and who conversed with dragons.

Yes, dragons.

I stepped out of the car and stared at the little house and shuddered. If I shifted my vision, I was pretty sure I knew what I'd See. Dragons with the ability to fry me to a crisp. Of course, if I didn't shift, they'd still be there. I just wouldn't see the blast coming. I decided to get a good look at what waited for me on the other side of the street.

A second and a heartbeat later and the urge to get back in the car and drive like hell was very strong.

Reneau's "dragons" were energy constructs, creatures that existed because she willed them to. Formed of her life force, or the life force of the whole neighborhood, and shaped by her will, the big lizards were the perfect protectors. She gave them all the power they needed to become sentient, and, in exchange, they looked after the homes of her neighborhood. The last time I visited, one large medieval-style dragon lay draped across the porch and dared anyone to be stupid enough to try anything. She never had issues with door-to-door salespeople.

Twelve dragons glared at me from the spine of the roof. And none of them looked happy.

I took a tentative step forward. Several of them roared in warning. To anyone else, it might've sounded like birds or even a train whistle as it went by on the nearby tracks. It sounded to me like giant monsters proclaiming lunch was served, and I was an appetizer.

"I wouldn't come any closer," called Reneau from the porch. She must've seen me coming. "Just get back in your car and leave."

"I need answers."

"I don't have any."

"They took my son."

She stared for a moment, then waved me across the street. Her spectral lizards bowed to their mistress and let me through the gate, but I felt her protective spells as I passed through. It was less a barrier than it was a crackle of electricity that singed the hair off my arm and took the lint off my jacket.

"You're on high alert," I said as I approached the porch.

"Who took your son?"

"I don't know," I said. "Someone murdered my mother and stole him. They left a mark..."

"Evergreen."

I nodded.

"Goddamn it. I thought that was all over and done with."

"How'd you know?"

"Because I'm not stupid," she said with a smirk. "You wouldn't be here otherwise. And I've heard rumblings."

A car drove past. Nothing I would pay attention to, but

she locked eyes with the driver and watched until it rounded the corner at the end of the block.

"Inside," she said. "Not safe out here."

A great deal can be gleaned about a person from looking at their living area. The things they keep, the colors they choose, the types of furniture they have, all say something about the type of person who lives there. Some people have more sports than art, more paintings than photos, others prefer fabric to leather.

And some people, like Reneau, seem to have a front room just to keep up appearances, and to act as an extra buffer to the outside world.

Everything in the front room looked as if it were torn from the pages of an old copy of Better Homes and Gardens. Antique chairs with a matching loveseat sat flanked by end tables with cut-glass lamps and lace doilies. Even the hardwood floor was protected by what appeared to be a large doily.

"Where do you hide the dungeon?"

She wasn't amused.

"I've been getting these for about a week now." She opened a drawer on one of the end tables and withdrew a small stack of envelopes. None had marks on them, but inside, each contained a single piece of paper. I unfolded the first. It was the Evergreen symbol.

"That one's in charcoal," she said. "One's done up in blood. There was one done up in shit, but I threw it out. Couldn't stand the smell."

"Wouldn't want it messing up your front room," I said. "Any idea who?"

"I distanced myself from Evergreen when Bill and Brea... When everything happened. I kept track of a few people, but I'm out of it now. I don't want anything to do with that name."

"Who else do you know of?"

"Blossom, but she doesn't want any part of them either. Bob..."

"Bob's dead." I didn't mean to just blurt it out, but the words fell out of my mouth before I could suck them back in. Once out, they lay like a fish on the antique table.

"How?" Reneau's face hardened into steely lines and anger.

"Something went to his church and sucked the life out of it, and him."

"That's not possible," she said. "Nothing could take that much energy..."

"There's more," I said. "I found out that Pittsburgh seems to have developed a vampire problem."

"What they do is their business." She gave a dismissive wave. "They've never bothered anyone before."

"Wait," I said as her words sunk in. "You knew about them?

For how long? How many are there?"

"They're harmless," she said. "They keep to themselves and the group of sycophantic followers that fawn over them."

"Yeah? Well, I got a visit a couple of nights ago from one of those harmless things, and it was something that came straight out of a nightmare. And now Andi's been infected with whatever makes a person a vampire."

"That's not my problem," she said. "If Bob's dead, and someone's looking at rebuilding Evergreen, we have much bigger issues."

Reneau's head snapped up at a sound. To me, it was the groan of a timber, the kind of noise a house made when it settled or shifted.

"Oh, Goddess," she whispered. "You need to leave. Now."

"Wait, what?"

She grabbed me by the collar and dragged me to the front door. Despite my best attempts to stop her, Reneau's will was iron and I couldn't break her grip. She threw the door open and froze.

On the doorstep lay the glittering remains of at least two of her dragons. And over them stood something that wasn't there. I saw where it should've been, where the air warped and moved around it. But I saw right through it, could see my car parked across the street behind it. It was darker than the rest of the porch, like shadow pooled together in a vague human shape, but it simply wasn't there.

But I could tell when it turned toward us.

"Oh, shit."

Reneau slammed the door and pushed me back through the house.

"Run," she said. "Out the back. Get out of here and find your kid."

"That thing knows where my son is!"

"That thing will kill you and suck the life out of you. It's not what stole your kid. It's a syphon."

I had no idea what she meant, but I was in no position to argue. I ran past the doorway into the rest of the house and into something out of a sadist's nightmare.

As I ran for what I hoped would be the back door, I caught glimpses of black leather, dark paint and wood, deep purples and cold steel. The rest of her house was a more accurate portrayal of the woman I knew as Reneau. So her husband knew, and obeyed her wishes to keep up appearances.

I found the back door and burst through to the outside, defenses up, such as they were. In the air, the cries and groans of Reneau's dragons echoed as they fought to defend their mistress. On the one hand, I wanted to help, to do anything to prevent a repeat of what happened to Bob. But, on the other hand, she was more powerful than me by buckets, didn't really like me, and would likely want me out of the way.

Also, I couldn't die. Not yet. I couldn't leave Daniel alone. I had to find him, and that meant survival, no matter how big a coward it made me feel.

The biggest problem was that my only method of escape, my car, sat parked across the street, and between me and it was this syphon thing, whatever that was. Not to mention Reneau's dwindling dragon force. I was blocked in by tall fences on all sides and hampered by my pudgy waistline and gimpy arm. No matter how I looked at things, I had to go through the gate, around to the front yard, across the street, into my car, and then drive away. And I had to do it without getting killed.

Reneau's fireworks on the front porch went beyond simple energy manipulation to manifest phenomena into the real world. What neighbors were home saw. As I crept along the side of the house, I glanced over to see an old woman, most likely on a stepladder, peer over the high fence to get a better glimpse of what was going on.

"Go back inside!" I hissed. "You want to die?"

"I'm calling the police!" She sounded more indignant than afraid.

"Good!" I whispered back. "Now get in the fucking house!"

The old woman disappeared in a huff. Reneau would have some serious damage control to do later to keep her place on the

HOA board.

If she survived.

I crept to the gate and listened. The air went silent. No more roars, no more crackle of energy. Just quiet. Then footsteps on the other side of the gate. I backed up and braced, ready to throw whatever I had at whatever came through the gate. The latch clicked and I coiled, ready to spring or run like hell the other way. The door flew open.

"What the hell are you still doing here?" Reneau was out of breath. Her face dripped with sweat. "I told you to get out of here. Go. Find your kid."

"What happened to the..?"

"I don't know," she said. "It just faded away. I don't know where it went, but it won't be gone long. Now go."

She grabbed me by the gimpy arm and dragged me through the gate and shoved me toward the road.

"Whoever's starting Evergreen again, whatever they want with your kid, it can't be good. You've got to find him."

"What about you?"

"What about me?" she said, like she took great offense. "Maggie wasn't the only strong witch around, you know. I can take care of—"

Her eyes went wide and her jaw hung open. For a moment, her whole body shuddered, then she drew in one long breath.

The inhalation continued, as she sucked in air and her body puckered. First the moisture from her fingers just vanished, then her arms. I recognized the result as the same way I found Bob in the church, desiccated and withered.

Behind her, the air warped and darkened.

The syphon.

I turned and ran. There was no room for pride, no place for bravery. There was no rational thought. There was only my survival, and the panic-stricken jolt that shocked my system into overdrive. I didn't bother to look back as I ran, certain that the syphon was behind me.

I tore through the gate and ran across the street without looking. A car slammed on its brakes, the driver cursed, but I made it into my car and, for some reason, I locked the doors.

Because, of course, plastic door locks were the perfect proof against a creature that sucked the life out of its victims.

As I jammed the key into the ignition, I chanced a look toward the house.

Every dragon Reneau created lay dissipating on the porch. The will that created them was gone, the energies that composed them, devoured.

At the back gate, Reneau's body hovered off the ground. Her gray skin flaked, dust against the sunlight. And behind her, the creature, or the bent light where the creature was, held her aloft and glared at me, as if it dangled her to taunt. Then it dropped her to the ground in a heap. It moved back toward the house. With my perception shifted, its intentions became clear. The house's energies, the dragons, everything that had to do with the power that once resided in the timbers, flowed toward the creature. It drank in the power, sucked it up like a snack.

I couldn't watch any more. The engine lurched as I stomped on the gas and sped down the street, leaving behind another black hole in a suburban tapestry.

12

I drove as fast as I could for the only safe place in Pittsburgh I knew: the shop.

To tell the truth, the drive to the shop was all a blur. How I managed to not hit someone, I don't know. But I don't remember the road. I don't remember turning the wheel or putting the car into the parking place. I don't remember putting the key in my pocket or walking through the back door. I don't even remember how I got on the floor of the workroom with Andi's cold arms around my shoulders.

Reneau's face, the startled horror on it, replayed over and over again in my mind. The cold anger, the determination, gone. All that was left in her eyes was fear. Child-in-the-dark fear. The kind that turns even the strongest people's nerves to jelly. That thing drained the life out of her right in front of me, and then drained her house. And it might have drained me too if she hadn't helped me escape.

I sobbed. I tried to describe what I saw to Andi, but the words just came out as a jumbled mess. There was nothing left in my mind but the absolute horror that something so insidious could exist, or even the revulsion that someone would call such a thing up on purpose.

"She said it was called a syphon," I said. "I don't even know what that is."

"Neither do I," said Andi. "But I'm going to find out."

My knowledge of the world of witchcraft is limited. I know that Magick comes down to energy manipulation and will, and I know that there are many different paths of witchcraft. Some follow the path of light. Others follow the "left-hand" path. There are hedge-witches, kitchen witches, solitaries, and covens. But for most of them, there are certain constants. One of the biggest, it seems, is that most every witch has what they call a "Book of Shadows." It sounds rather dramatic, but what it boils down to is a journal in which they keep spells, progress, thoughts, recipes, and anything else they feel needs to be recorded. The way most of them regard it, a Book of Shadows is a huge, leather-bound tome that radiates energy and should never fall into the wrong hands.

Maggie's was a ten-subject spiral notebook decorated with heart stickers. It more resembled a junior high schoolgirl's class composition book than a powerful repository of knowledge. But the energy she'd placed in it was palpable. Every spell she knew, every charm she made, was meticulously documented within its pages. There was a section for rituals, another for ointments, and others I didn't understand, but they were important to her. In the back, there was a section without a label. In it were notes in no particular order. There were entries about scats, the rat demons we faced, her favorite date with me, and other topics that had no correlation. Her most private thoughts were there on paper, her soul laid bare. It seemed like a violation to read it, and it made me miss her all the more.

Andi skimmed the pages as I tried not to think about the hands that had written the words.

"I don't see anything about a syphon," she said. "But I did find this."

She lifted two loose envelopes from the notebook. Both were sealed, made from different paper. And one had my name on it, written in her lovely script. The other had "Daniel" written across the front.

"Looks like letters for her boys," she said as she handed them to me.

"Yeah." I held the letters in my hand, curious about what was in them but afraid to find out.

"Aren't you going to open them?"

"Not now," I said as I took the notebook. I tucked the notes back between the pages and put the spiral back on the shelf. Whatever was in them would have to wait until later. Until after I found Daniel.

I turned to go back toward the car and stumbled over my feet. Andi caught me with frightening speed.

"Hey," she said. "You okay?"

"Fine."

She gave me an appraising look.

"When was the last time you slept?"

It was a simple question, and one I should've been able to answer. But, for the life of me, I couldn't remember. Before my mother went into the hospital, or after? My eyelids suddenly gained substantial weight as I realized how tired I was.

"Don't know," I said. "Don't have time to sleep. I need to find Daniel."

"You're not going to find anyone except death if you try to drive like this," she said. "You need to get some sleep. At least a couple of hours."

"But…"

"Look," she said. "Sun's going down. I can go out and look. You need to get some sleep."

"Fine," I said. "But are you sure?"

"I'll be fine," she said. "I've got a couple of blood packs left. I won't hurt anyone. You can trust me."

"Fine," I said again. "Maybe a nap would be good."

"Make sure he sleeps," said Andi to the shop. "He doesn't leave until he gets some sleep."

The walls shuddered in response. Great. I had a city block for a babysitter.

"Upstairs," she said. "March. Go to bed."

I begrudgingly did as she asked. Even as I was being forced into it, the thought of sleep wasn't so bad. But there was another reason I didn't want to sleep.

The apartment was too cold. Not temperature-wise, but emotionally. Everywhere I turned, Maggie's things stared at me, demanded to know when their mistress would return. The little witch figures that adorned her kitchen window, the vast array of teacups on the bar. On the stove sat a teapot that would never be used again. It was hers. Everything in the apartment was hers. We had lived together, but the only things in the apartment that were mine were the clothes that hung in my side of the closet, and I couldn't bear to open the door because her clothes still hung there too.

I walked through to the bedroom and opened the door. The empty crib made the hopeless melancholy worse. The two people who really needed to be there were gone, and all that was left was me. Even the bed seemed hard, uninviting, without her.

I turned around and went back to the living room and lay

down on the couch. As I stared at the ceiling, Bitsy hopped up on my stomach and lay down. She missed Maggie too. I was sure of it.

I closed my eyes and petted Bitsy's head as exhaustion overrode my intention and claimed me. My last thought before I drifted off was how much I hoped I wouldn't dream.

I awoke several hours later, as the first rays of the sun filtered through the blinds, and felt a little clearer-headed. At least I could think straight. I stumbled toward the bathroom for a shower to wake me the rest of the way. While the water poured over my head, a plan took shape in my mind.

Well, less a plan than it was a broad outline of things that I needed to do.

I needed to touch base with Norman to find out if the Pittsburgh Police Department had managed to find anything out, though I doubted they would. After that, I needed to contact Blossom, the only surviving member of the core of Evergreen that I knew of. Although she didn't strike me as the sort that would kidnap my kid, I needed to be sure, and at least give her a heads-up about the syphon. And maybe find out if she knew anything useful I could use against it.

I came out of the shower to find Bitsy in the middle of the bed. In front of her sat the two envelopes from Maggie. As much as I wanted to, I couldn't. Not yet. My heart ached to see them, but I had to focus. Too much yet to do.

"Later," I said to the cat. She snorted her disapproval.

My first stop was to see if Andi had made any progress. To my surprise, the back door to the shop was unlocked, but a heavy tarp hung in the doorway. I pushed it aside and stepped in. Andi greeted me with a smile.

"Feel better?"

"Yeah," I said. "You let me sleep too long."

"You needed it."

"Sun's up," I said. "Aren't you supposed to be, I don't know, asleep or something?"

"Like in a coffin?" She snorted. "I just need to stay out of direct sunlight. The tarp keeps it out of here, and she keeps the front windows blacked out. I can keep up with the business if I need to."

"What about..?"

"Food? Still working on that part."

I nodded. No matter what, vampire or not, Andi was still Andi. She deserved my trust and my love.

"I have to go," I said. "I wish you could come with me."

"Sunlight's not my friend," she said. "Not anymore."

"Who're you kidding?" I grinned. "When was the last time you went outdoors in the daylight anyway?"

"Fair point." She stuck her tongue out at me and for one moment, things were like they were. Just me and the kid, a weird relationship based on mutual antagonism and lighthearted ribbing.

Pittsburgh, like a lot of other cities, has a lot of cultural points of interest. The museums are things of beauty to behold, and the Phipps Garden Center is a must-see for the botanically inclined. I'm more of an animal person—or at least I was until my untimely demise.

I had spent a fair bit of time in the National Aviary before I died, when I was normal. Same for the Pittsburgh Zoo. Those days, however, came to an abrupt end after I visited the Aviary after I died and the birds went insane when they caught a whiff of me. Something about my recent return from the other side spooked them. I didn't fare too much better at the zoo either. I set foot in the observation areas and normally docile animals got very aggressive. Aggressive animals went into full-blown panic mode. Ever since I died and came back, almost every animal I came into contact with reacted with fear. Even domesticated animals, dogs, most cats, ran when I came into the room. I tried really hard to stay away from the zoo and from any animal other than Bitsy.

But it was an emergency, and I was desperate. Though the

kidnapper had made no demands yet, I couldn't shake the feeling that I was running out of time.

The crowd was light for autumn, and it was early enough in the morning that there weren't too many people for me to encounter. Too often, interactions with me led to gawkers and well-meaning Samaritans on their cell phones with the police. I walked to the turnstile and reached for my wallet.

"I'm not stupid, you know."

Officer Norman waved from the ticket booth. The other guy waved me through as Norman came out and greeted me.

"What're you doing here?"

"Might ask you the same thing," he said. "But I already know the answer. You're looking for other members of Evergreen to find out what they know about your missing kid, right?"

"Yeah."

"Well," he said. "Let's go. Who's here?"

"You don't know?"

"Evergreen, the group, is known to the police, but the members aren't. We know a few aliases, a few places of business, but no real names."

"Blossom," I said. "Earth-mother type. Loves animals. She's the last of the old Evergreen core that I know. I need to get to her before someone else does."

"Like who?"

I wanted to trust Norman, even though most people I trusted ended up dead or betrayed me. Something told me he wouldn't, though. Maybe it was the ghost of Taylor acting like my guardian angel on my shoulder, or even wishful thinking.

"I doubt she took my son, but someone might be coming for her."

"How do you know that?"

"Did you get a call to a residence in Fox Chapel? Woman named Kim?"

He nodded.

"I knew her as Reneau. Something called a syphon came after her. I don't know what it is, but it killed her. Drained all of her power out."

"Someone's killing old Evergreen and rebuilding it?"

"That's what I'm thinking," I said. "I just wish I knew how Daniel fit into their plans."

We walked in tense silence until we reached the kangaroo habitat. It was the last place I knew she worked, and she loved the weird creatures. As we approached, every animal in sight went on high alert.

"Can I help you?" One of the keepers approached. He looked just as spooked as his animals.

"We're looking for..."

It occurred to me that I didn't actually know if Blossom

was her real name or not. Some of the members of Evergreen didn't see the point in secret names while others adhered to the old Pagan rule of secrecy. Half the time, it was obvious. The rest, it seemed rude to ask. For all I knew, her parents were hippies.

"Blossom?"

"Around back," he said. "And hurry up. You're freaking out my babies." He pointed around the cage toward an outbuilding.

Norman and I made our way to the building and knocked on the door.

"Who is it?" I recognized the voice, but it was more strained than I remembered.

"Pittsburgh P.D.," said Norman. "We'd like to ask you a few questions."

"Got a warrant?" The voice was testy, not Blossom's usual mellow tone.

"Um... No, ma'am," he said. "But..."

"Then fuck off," she shouted. "I don't have to talk to you."

"Blossom, it's me," I said. "Stan Cooper."

A few seconds of silence followed.

"Stan? Is it really you?"

"It's me," I said.

The locks clicked and the door creaked open. The woman who opened the door didn't look like the friendly Earth-mother I remembered. It was Blossom, all right, but her long hair was disheveled, her face glistened with sweat. She looked like she hadn't slept in days. She motioned us inside, then locked the door behind us.

"So, I take it you heard about Reneau?"

Blossom nodded as tears rushed down her cheeks.

"Whoever did this, they took my son, killed my mom. The thing they used to take out Reneau and Bob was something called a syphon."

What color was left in Blossom's face drained out.

"How do you know that?"

"Reneau told me," I said. "Right before it killed her."

"A syphon. You're sure that's what she said."

I nodded. She let out a long breath and sat down on a bench.

"A syphon is pretty much what the name implies," she said. "It sucks the living energy out of one vessel and puts it into another. Like sucking the gas out of one car and putting it into someone else's tank. The source dies, but the receiver adds years and power."

"Who could've called it?" Norman pulled his notebook out of his inside pocket. Sometimes the guy could be a walking cliché.

"Nobody," she said. "Not that I know of. The power it takes to create one of those things is insane, and it's really black Magick.

Everyone I know of who could have conjured one is dead."

"How can I kill it?"

Blossom shook her head and shrugged.

"I've never encountered one," she said. "I only know about them because I like reading old texts. Everything I ever read about them just said to avoid them at all costs."

"Any idea why someone would want to send it after you and the rest of Evergreen?"

Blossom dipped her head and stared at her shoes.

"There were factions," she said. "Members who thought that, since we were more powerful than the average people, we should take advantage of it. Some of them thought we betrayed the Goddess by allowing open discourse about religion. They wanted to purge Evergreen. A pure Evergreen."

"A ruling class," I said. She nodded.

"I need names," said Norman. "Addresses if you have them."

"Bill and Brea were the main two," she said. "And they're dead. They're all dead. Oh, Goddess, I'm the last one left."

Fresh tears rolled down her face.

"Come with us," I said. "The police, they can protect you."

"No they can't," she wailed. "You know that better than anyone else. They can't protect me, and the syphon is coming for me."

"Hey!" I took her shoulders and knelt to her eye level. "We're trying to help," I said. "Isn't there anyone?"

"No," she sniffed. "But if they're really going to resurrect Evergreen, this is the way to do it. Fresh start, clear out the old dead wood. Hell, I'm surprised they didn't come for me first."

"What do they want with Daniel? What are they going to do to him?"

"Best guess? Innocent blood. Consecration. It's very dark Magick, and not something I like being involved with."

"We've got to find him," I said. "I need to find my son."

"Better be quick," she said. "Once I'm gone, he's the last step, I'd bet."

Outside, the animals shrieked and howled. Cages rattled as if the doors might come off.

"It's here," said Blossom. All trace of fear was gone from her voice. The only thing that remained was razor-edged anger.

I was used to seeing the warm smile, the love that radiated out to all living things. To be honest, I had never thought of Blossom as the type who would harm so much as a gnat. But her eyes hardened, her mouth tightened, and she radiated more cold hatred than I ever believed possible.

"You two get out of here," she said, eyes on the door. "There's a back way out. Use it."

"You can't stay," said Norman. "It'll kill you. We need to get you somewhere safe."

"It'll hurt my animals," she said. "And I won't allow that. If it wants me, by the Goddess, it's going to get me."

I didn't need to switch my sight. The energy poured off of her in waves of rage and heat. Norman winced as he felt it too.

"Whatever happens," she said. "Find that baby. You've got to find him. Don't let them hurt him."

Norman and I didn't wait for further instructions. We ran toward the back door, unlatched it, and ran through.

For a moment, I had a vision of us coming out into some insanely dangerous situation, like maybe the gorilla paddock, where three big silverbacks stared at us, as if they wanted to know just what the hell we thought we were doing in their neck of the jungle. Maybe we would be trapped between dangers.

Instead, we wound up face to face with the syphon.

Sad, really. I would've rather had my arms torn off by a gorilla.

Norman gaped at what he saw and drew his gun.

"Pittsburgh P.D!" he shouted.

The warped air of where the thing stood rippled. I could swear it laughed. Then the thing took a step toward us.

Norman's gun barked four times as the muzzle flashed. Dirt sprayed up behind the syphon where the bullets hit the ground, but it kept coming. I blinked and shifted my vision to see it better.

In the technicolor tapestry of the zoo, the warp in the fabric of the world glowed pure energy, neither good nor bad. Just energy, directed by an outside force. A puppet, connected to its master by a straw through which he or she fed. But instead of warped air, I saw its shape, saw it for what it was. The thing looked like a man, but without the physical form to tie it to the world. It had a current, almost like it had a life force without a real consciousness to guide it.

Which meant that the person who controlled it was still attached to it. I hoped I was right.

I willed power into my dead arm. The ruined tattoo flared blue and leaped to life as my ghost arm took shape. My first thought was to try to flood it with energy, but I didn't know how much it could eat. It had already drained one of the most powerful witches around and seemed still hungry. Little old me wouldn't be much of a snack for it.

But then it occurred to me that maybe the straw went both ways.

I visualized the energy of the syphon, grabbed it, took hold and pulled hard. The creature shuddered, then it staggered. Raw power coursed out of it and into my arm, into my body, filled up my core with more energy than I knew what to do with.

Images slammed into my mind, movement in the dark, a

pair of man's hands with dirty nails, clenched in agony, brown sleeves. In the corner of whatever room I saw sat a bassinet, and in it Daniel slept.

"He's alive!"

Norman spared a glance toward me, but continued to fire at the wraith. It did no good, but he fired just the same, as if to not do so would be the crazy thing.

I pulled harder, yanked the fishing line and reeled, so I could see more details. Something had to be there, some clue to tell me where Daniel was, how to find him. Grey floors, wood walls, nothing of significance stood out. Until the person's vision panned past a framed picture on a wall. Beside it was a lamp, and beside that, a fireplace. I recognized it. From the chipped stonework to the dollar-ninety-nine picture frame, I knew where he was.

The energy straw snapped tight, and pain lanced through my head. Whoever it was knew I'd seen him, and he wasn't too happy about the invasion. The syphon vanished and took all the heat energy out of the air with it.

Norman made a slow revolution, gun poised, eyes wide.

"What the hell was that?"

"Syphon," I said. "That's what got Reneau."

"Son of a bitch," he panted. "Bullets go right through it."

"I noticed. I also noticed you kept shooting."

He snapped his eyes to mine, then managed to look pissed and sheepish at the same time.

"I didn't know what else to do," he muttered.

"We need to go," I said. "I know where he is. Blossom!"

There was no answer. A cold ache crept into the pit of my stomach.

"Blossom?"

Norman pushed the door to the shed open. She lay on the floor, desiccated and empty. While we fought with the syphon, something else got to her. Maybe a second syphon, maybe some other evil thing. I couldn't tell. All I knew was another person I considered, if not a friend, an ally lay dead, and I couldn't stop it.

"God damn it," said Norman. "I need to call this in."

"In the car," I said. "We've got to go. Now."

A low noise started as we opened the door, a mournful bay that I couldn't at first identify. The animals in their cages stood by the bars, as close as they could to the walking path. Many bowed their heads. Others stood on their hind legs and pointed their snouts skyward. All of them howled.

13

Past the Fort Pitt tunnel, the exit to the suburb of Green Tree sat quiet and innocuous. There wasn't really much to it, a nature center and a few parks. In fact, wholly unremarkable to the unknowing person. But to me, Green Tree was ominous, a place where unspeakable evil lurked just beneath the surface.

Of course, that could be because two of its inhabitants had tried to kill me and take over the world. I tended to lump people in with their neighbors.

"The house is up there." I pointed up the mountainside. "They liked their privacy."

We turned up the gravel road and switched back up the steep grade. When we came to the gate, I was surprised to find it stood open.

Norman checked the clip in his gun and nodded.

The further up the road the car crept, the darker it seemed to be, until we parked in front of what used to be the home of Bill and Brea, two batshit-crazy mages who had fancied themselves benevolent gods to rule over humanity.

Until I killed them.

Norman shut off the engine and got out, gun in hand. The urge to sprint to the door and kick it down was strong, but so was the desire to stay alive and not walk into a trap. I decided to go with the second and crept to the front porch with Norman, gun raised, in tow.

The door stood open.

"No..."

Norman pushed the door wide and we stared into the darkness. Less than a year since Bill and Brea welcomed me and Maggie into their home, smiled and took us in as friends, all the while intending to sacrifice me, and the place still looked the same. At least, what I could see did. Maybe a bit dustier.

I triggered my second sight and gaped. The whole house should've shone like a nuclear power plant. But where there should have been some trace of power, a signature of energy, an imprint at least, there was nothing. No afterimages, no residue, nothing to indicate anything, animal or vegetable, had ever lived in the house, let alone two crazy wizards. The whole of what I could see was sucked clean of every last bit of dark energy.

"Keep looking," I said. "There's got to be something left."

Norman nodded and proceeded into the house. As he

passed from room to room, he called out "clear" when he found nothing. I limited my search to the room I saw in the vision. The living room. The framed photo, the lamp, the fireplace, they all belonged to Bill and Brea. The photo showed the members of Evergreen in happier times. Before I met them. Before they died.

"Nothing," said Norman as he reentered the room and put his gun away. "If he was here, he's gone now."

"Of course he is," I said. "He saw us coming. Now he's moved and I have no way of knowing where he went."

"What do you want to do?"

I kicked at the carpet for a second. What I wanted to do was hold my son in my arms. But I couldn't. I was at a loss. Every member of Evergreen that I knew was dead, which meant the killer was either done, or he was coming for me next. I hoped for the latter.

"Home," I said. "I need to check on Andi. Maybe she'll have an idea of what to do."

"Like a tracking spell or something?"

"I don't know," I said. "I hope so."

My father once told me that good things happen when a person least suspects them. Blessings in disguises, he called them, or even happenstance.

"Sometimes," he said, "you have to stop pushing so hard

and just let things unfold."

Dad was smart. Not book-smart, but he had a lot more common sense and world knowledge than anyone I knew. When I was a kid, I always looked to him for wisdom. When he died, I missed his advice.

We pulled up at the shop and parked. The front windows were still tinted black, but the door stood a little open. The shop was open for business, it seemed.

Norman let me out of the car and, after questioning me for the hundredth time about whether or not I was okay, headed back to the station. Paperwork, he said, or some such thing. I didn't really pay attention because I was too busy kicking myself for being such an idiot. Of course he saw us coming. I practically gave whoever it was a wedgie and may as well have played the William Tell Overture to announce our arrival.

As I walked through the back door and pushed past the curtain, voices caught my attention. I knew the first one as Andi. The second, I thought I recognized, but couldn't place it right away.

"I'm not really sure when he'll be back," said Andi. "He's attending to some business right now."

"I need to see him," said the mystery woman. "I'm a friend."

"I know all of his friends." Andi's voice tightened. "I don't know you."

"We just met..."

The lock on the front door snapped shut as I pushed through the curtain to see a defensive-looking Andi facing off across the counter from a determined-looking Lily Fitch.

"I see you two have met," I said. "Andrea Bedford, meet Lily Fitch. Artist. Lily, this is Andi. Business partner and overprotective friend."

"Can you blame me?" Andi flashed angry eyes at me.

"Oh, thank God you're okay," said Lily. "Are you okay? What's happened? Something's happened, hasn't it?"

"Calm down," I said. "A lot's happened."

It only took about five minutes to give her the highlights. Baby kidnapped, mom dead, Evergreen resurfacing, and a thing called a syphon on the loose. Not to mention that there were vampires in Pittsburgh. When I was done, I half-expected her to run and never look back. Instead, she pulled her sketchpad from her backpack.

"I knew something was going on," she said. "I didn't know how bad it was. Can I help in any way?"

"We've got it covered, thanks." Andi bristled every time Lily offered assistance.

"Actually," I said. "I could use all the help I can get. I don't know where they've taken my son, and I don't have any way of finding out. Then there's Andi..."

"Hey!"

"... and the vampire that attacked her. There's too much going on and I can't focus on anything."

"How'd you know to come here, anyway?" Andi leaned forward off her stool. "Awfully convenient, you showing up right when bad things happen, isn't it?" Before she was bitten, she could be intimidating. After, she was downright terrifying.

Lily flipped her sketchpad open and held it out to us.

"I see things," she said. "Visions. Sometimes they come true, other times they don't. But I see them, all the same."

The first page was almost completely covered in black, save for a slightly lighter outline of a girl in the corner of a room. The shop's back room, to be precise. Where the eyes of the girl would be, two white dots in the dark charcoal marks stared out. It was Andi, the night she came home.

I flipped the page to find the wheel of my mother's car, a boot-clad leg next to it.

Page three showed me with a nightmare of a creature over me. I recognized it as the vampire I had seen. Above it were strings, and a cloaked figure to pull them.

The scene on the fourth page showed what appeared to be Bob, Blossom, and Reneau. Out of them flew their souls. And over them stood a great open mouth that swallowed them in a vortex of darkness.

"You saw all of this?"

She nodded.

"Or she caused it all," muttered Andi.

"That's enough," I said. "Excuse us for a moment."

I took Andi by the arm and dragged her through to the back of the shop. In hindsight, it probably wasn't the smartest thing to do, seeing as she was stronger than me and if she got hungry enough, could tear my arms off and suck the meat out of them. But she let me guide her to the workroom.

"What is your problem?"

"Who the hell is she?"

"I met her the other night, outside your vampire club."

"Right," said Andi. "You just met her. You don't know her. So why are you trusting her?"

I didn't have a good answer. Hell, I didn't even have a bad answer. All I knew was that I did and it didn't matter why.

"Look, do you trust me?"

"Of course I do," she snapped. "It's her I don't trust."

"Great," I said. "You don't have to trust her. I'm not asking you to trust her. Trust me. I trust her, and you should know by now that my trust doesn't come easy."

"But..."

"I can't explain it," I said. "I just do. It's a gut feeling, okay? Now will you please just play nice? What the hell is wrong with you, anyway?"

"I'm hungry," she said. "I need to feed."

A cold chill shot up my spine and settled under my hair.

"Oh," I said. I took a step toward the refrigerator.

"It's empty," said Andi. "I finished it all while you were out. Then she showed up. Gods, Stan. I'm so hungry."

"Keep calm," I said. "I'll call Norman. See if I can get some more blood from the hospital."

"Better hurry," she said. "It's getting hard to push it down."

The problem with Andi's hunger was that, while she could suppress it through Magick, that Magick took energy from her body, which she needed to replenish with food, which meant it made her more hungry. In other words, if she tried to suppress it, it only made the hunger worse. She needed to feed, and soon. I didn't like the alternatives.

I made my way back through the curtain. Lily stood at the counter, sketchbook in one hand, pencil in the other. Her eyes were closed and her lips moved. The pencil flew across the page so fast it seemed impossible that anything would come out more than a random scribble.

"Lily?"

Her eyes snapped open,for a moment confused, then took a good long look at her sketchbook.

"Is this your son?"

The likeness was uncanny. I nodded.

"He's alive," she said. "I can see him. I can't see where he is, but I can see him. He's alive."

"How do you know?" Andi glowered from the back room entrance.

"Like I said. I see things."

"Is there a way for you be able to see where he is?" Hope landed on my shoulder. I wasn't about to shoo it away. "Like deep meditation or something?"

"I don't know," she said. "It doesn't work that way. I see what I see. I can't control it."

"Which makes it useless for us," snarled Andi. She snatched up her backpack from under the counter and headed toward the back of the shop.

"Where're you going?"

"It's dark," she snapped. "I'm going out. Maybe I can get a handle on at least one of our problems."

"Andi..."

"Believe me, you don't want me here right now."

The back heavy curtain parted and the back door opened in front of her, then slammed and locked behind her as she stormed out.

"I'm sorry," said Lily after an awkward pause. "I didn't mean... Is she your..?"

"No," I said. "She's a friend and business partner. That's all. She's defensive. She was friends with Daniel's mother."

"I'm so sorry," she said. Another awkward pause. "Look... You look like you haven't eaten in a while. You hungry?"

It didn't occur to me until she mentioned it, but I couldn't remember the last time I actually ate. I remembered the beer I had shared with the freaky doll in my apartment, but beyond that, nothing of substance had hit my belly in a while.

"Yeah," I said. "I guess I am."

"C'mon. On me."

Food has quite a significant place in human history and folklore. Whenever great men and women meet, there is always food present. Wine and cheese and cakes are important in Pagan traditions. Hell, even the Last Supper springs to mind. Food, for whatever reason, resonates with people. It's why house parties always end up in the kitchen, and why weddings always need two overpriced cakes to commemorate the occasion. Everyone remembers the first meal with a new lover. And inmates on death row get a last meal. Food is important.

Lots of folks come to Pittsburgh for the food. We have great Italian food, fantastic Greek food, even a whole section of town dedicated to the worship of fresh bread and pasta. We even have a place that brings in fresh fish by the boatload, and makes the best crab cakes anyone's ever had. But for me, the simple places work best.

Primanti Bros. doesn't feature haute cuisine or a wine list or fancy tables. As restaurants go, it's pretty lowbrow. Every wall features big-screen televisions that show hockey or the fights, and the whole place is put together more like a clubhouse than a restaurant. It's bar food. Wonderful, glorious bar food.

And that was why it was my favorite place to eat.

We sat and ordered. Beer and a gyro for me, beer and a pulled pork sandwich for her. Then we sat in silence for a few minutes and stared at our glasses.

"Thank you," I said. "For this. I can't remember the last time I ate."

"I figured as much," she said. "Andi. She was the one who... at the club?"

"Yeah. You'll have to excuse her. She doesn't trust easily. Plus there's that whole new-to-bloodlust thing."

"I don't blame her," said Lily with a shrug. "I'm guessing she was close to your ex?"

My "ex." I didn't really consider Maggie my "ex." I more considered myself widowed, though we were never officially married. Maybe it was because she meant more to me than the word "wife" could ever mean.

"You could say that."

Close didn't begin to describe them. Besties, maybe? Sisters? Half the time I didn't know if Andi considered Maggie a mother or a mentor. Or both. She took Maggie's death almost as hard as I did, but where I ran, she held Daniel closer. The whole vampirism thing only made matters worse.

"What was she like? Maggie, I mean."

"Why do you care?" It came out harder than I wanted, but was still a legitimate question.

"Because it's obvious you and Andi loved her very much. I just would like to know why."

Our food came, and between bites, I told her stories of Maggie, told her of our lives together. About the time I tried to cut my own hair and she had to fix it. About the time I gave up being a stubborn asshole and admitted I loved her. I told her about how Maggie had lived. And how she died. It didn't seem weird or awkward at all. Just two friends discussing a third. I even caught myself in the middle of a laugh once or twice. At least I didn't fall down crying into my tzatziki sauce.

"She sounds like someone I would've liked to have known," she said. "I think I would've liked her."

"Yeah. Everyone who knew her liked her. She was kind of amazing like that."

"Let me help you find your son," she said. "Let me at least try. I can't do much but I'll do whatever I can."

"Thank you," I said. "I'll take whatever help I can get. It means a lot to me."

14

Whether it was the food that recharged my batteries or the conversation that sparked my mind, my brain kicked in and started to function like it was supposed to. Sure, Lily may have been a psychic, but that didn't mean she was the only source of information at hand. There were always other, more conventional methods of investigation. And I had at least one cop who wanted to be part of whatever I had going on.

"Shannon," I said into my phone. "I need a favor."

"You got it!" I pictured him bouncing up and down with excitement.

"The house in Green Tree. I need to know who owns it."

"Way ahead of you," he said. "I've been running a check since we got back. Records show that, after William Keith was declared dead, the house and entire estate went up for auction. The whole lot was bought by an anonymous bidder."

Damn.

"I need to know who that bidder was."

"I figured," he said. "I've got some people working on it." By "people," I guessed he meant himself and an unpaid intern.

"Let me know what you find out." I said, then hung up.

"Now what?" Lily glanced from her food and back, half nervous, half fascinated.

I explained to her over dinner that the building was alive. Even more, I explained how it came to be that way. Magick was real, I had died and come back, and so on. She took it better than I thought she would, and only said no way once before she decided she believed me.

"We need to find Andi," I said. "Make sure she's still doing alright."

"Shouldn't we wait until she comes back?"

"It's probably the safest option," I said. "But what if she does something she'd regret in the meantime? Andi's not a killer. Right now, she might feel like one, but I think if she actually did kill someone, it would destroy her."

"Okay," she said. "Where do we look?"

"Where else?"

Back in the day, I really thought it was cool to go to clubs so often that the doormen knew my name. The doorperson at Nocturnity, however, I wished would forget it.

"Mister Cooper," she said. "Back again?"

"Looking for someone," I growled. "Tell your boss I need to talk to him again."

The doorperson glared at Lily for a moment.

"Don't I know you?" Then, as recognition flared in her eyes. "Don't you draw stuff on the sidewalk outside?"

"She's with me," I said as I stepped between them. "You got a problem with that?"

"I'll let Mister Ravenwood know you're here," she said. "If you'd like to wait at the bar."

Lily looked out of place, a cute bohemian in a room full of Goths. In fact, she looked a little disoriented by the red lights and ear-splitting music. But she smiled at me as we took seats at the bar. A young person (male or female, I couldn't tell which due to long hair, heavy makeup and unisex clothing) brought us both drinks.

"Compliments of Mister Ravenwood," they shouted over the din.

"Just water," I shouted back. "Where is he?"

"He'll be right down," shouted the bartender. "I'm afraid he's speaking to another customer at the moment."

Before I could think of a witty retort, glass shattered from above, and a chair crashed to the floor. Part of me knew what I'd see when I looked up, but didn't want to admit it.

The office window was devoid of glass, and in the empty frame stood Andi, her eyes white in the red light. Ravenwood cowered before her, all pretense of vampire supremacy gone by the wayside.

"Andi!"

She stopped and stared down at us, her face a mask of hatred and fury. Then her eyes shifted to Lily, and what had been anger morphed into hurt.

I ran for the staircase and hurried up to the office, Lily in tow. The door hung off one hinge.

"Andi?"

She turned and stared at me. The little girl I knew, the spunky, punky teen I pulled out of the trunk of a car not so long ago, was gone. What stood in her place was terrifying. Her hands ended in wicked claws that were painted black. Her pale skin lightened to alabaster, and looked almost as hard as marble. She seemed less related to the human race than to the creature outside my door only days ago.

"Walk away, Stan," she said. "This fucker knows what did this to me, and he's going to tell me."

"Please!" he shrieked. "I don't know anything! Jesus Christ, please! Oh, God!"

"Shut up!" she hissed.

"Andi! This isn't you!" I tried to remember everything I'd

seen in movies and television about talking a psycho down. None of it seemed to relate. "You're not a monster. You do this, you won't be able to live with yourself."

"I can't live with myself now! All I want to do is eat! I want to kill everyone around me! You don't know what it's like to be turned into a monster! He knows what did this! It's his club! He has to know!"

She took a step toward him. Ravenwood crumpled into an even smaller ball.

"Is that what Maggie would've wanted?" Lily's voice cut through the dubstep and screams. I turned, stunned that she not only spoke, but that she mouthed off to a pissed-off vampire who already didn't like her.

"What did you say?" Andi turned, lips curled into a sneer.

"Is this what Maggie would've wanted you to do? Give in? Become a killer?"

"Don't you dare say her name!" screamed Andi. She lunged, claws directed toward Lily's eyes. But while her attention was on Lily, she didn't see me react.

I keep a talisman with me. Really, it's nothing more than a little pewter figure that I keep on my keyring. But, to me, it's much more than that. It's a symbol of love and I like to think it keeps me safe when my own stupidity would lead me to another untimely demise. It's a small, rustic goddess figure. It's great to use as an energy focus.

And it was a gift from Maggie.

As Andi made for Lily's eyes, I slapped the figure against her forehead and pushed. It took less time than a blink, but the effect, even without my perception shifted, was spectacular.

The spot where it touched her burst into light that thrust the room into a moment of pure white agony, then she collapsed, unconscious. The monster was again the girl I knew.

"Holy... Holy shit!" Ravenwood scrambled up off the floor. "She was going to kill me! She was really going to kill me!"

"Shut up," I said. "I came to ask you the same question."

"But... you saved me! Oh my God, thank you! You saved my life!"

"I didn't do it for you," I said. "I did it for her."

It took a few minutes of tense words and not-so-subtlly implied threats to convince Ravenwood to not call the police or file a report. In the end, I played on his knowledge of vampire lore to convince him that, if he tried to put her in jail, she'd turn into smoke, flit through the bars, and eat his face. Of course, I couldn't be sure, but I didn't think vampires could actually turn into smoke. Or bats. Or do half the crazy stuff folklore said they could. But they could do two things very well. They could scare the hell out of anyone, and they could kill.

After a few more minutes of Marx-brothers level idiocy, we figured out how to get Andi back to the shop. As small as she was, she was difficult for a one-armed man to carry, and too heavy for Lily alone. In the end, to save her dignity, we wound up looping one arm over my neck and one over Lily's. We walked her out like a drunk after a frat party.

Someone did call the police. In fact, multiple someones due to the immediate accessibility of their cell phones, but, with a bit of coaching from me, Ravenwood put on a good show of saying it was all an act to drum up business. A vampire-themed bar with real vampires? Who could resist, right?

Once back in the shop, it took a little more explaining as to why the building shook. But I reminded her that, not only was the building alive, but we were carrying its mother like we killed her. Lily seemed to accept my explanation like it was the most normal thing in the world. We gently placed Andi in Maggie's summoning circle and traced the outline of it with salt. When she woke up, I was pretty sure she'd be pissed off, but I hoped the salt would make her stay put.

"You know they're going to use the videos from tonight for marketing," said Lily. "Right?"

I snorted. Of course they would.

"Ravenwood doesn't know anything about the thing that made Andi," I said.

"How do you know?"

"He's a coward. The way she came after him? He'd have talked if he knew anything."

"You're sure?"

"Absolutely," I said. "Trust me, he's not our guy."

"Then we're back at square one."

"We?"

"I'm here, aren't I?" Lily smiled. "I said I wanted to help."

"Why? You barely even know me."

"Because I can," she said with a shrug. "Because you're kind, and I can see it. And because I want to. Isn't that enough?"

Any other situation, any other person, it might sound creepy, or at least a little mental. But, for some reason I couldn't fathom, I trusted her. I wanted to trust her. So I did.

Andi let out a low groan. For a moment, terror gripped my guts as I didn't know which Andi would wake up, the girl or the monster.

"Jesus, Stan," she said as she rolled onto her back. "What happened to me?"

On her forehead was the burned outline of the goddess figure I used to put her out. If I was lucky, it would fade before she noticed it. If not, she had another interesting body mod and a story to tell, if she didn't decide to murder me in my sleep for it.

"What do you remember?"

"Everything," she said. "But I remember it all being a really good idea at the time." She opened her eyes and sat up.

Lily did her best to stay very small behind me.

"You." Andi sounded more annoyed and tired than angry. "You baited me into attacking."

"Yeah," said Lily. "Sorry."

"Ballsy," said Andi. "Stupid, but ballsy."

"Stan had my back."

"I see that," she said. Andi ran her hands through her hair and rubbed her face, but stopped when she touched the mark on her forehead. "What... What the hell..?"

"Now... Before you get angry..." I said.

"MIRROR!"

Turned out the whole vampires-can't-see-themselves-in-mirrors thing wasn't true. She saw the mark very well. So well, in fact, that her rage lasted only until she decided it looked "punk" and she wanted to keep it.

"Stan," she said. "Look, I'm in control again, but I'm still hungry. Like, really hungry. If I don't get blood soon, I'm going to go all vampy-bitch again."

"I'm working on it," I said.

The walls shook and the temperature dropped by at least ten degrees in the span of a heartbeat. Andi's head snapped toward the door.

"Oh, shit," she said.

From the other side of the door, I heard an all-too-familiar sound, a growl with inhuman vocal cords. The last time I had heard it so close, it was on the other side of the apartment door.

"I can hear it," said Andi. "In my head. I can feel it."

"Can you see the person holding it?"

"No," she said. "But I can feel its hate. Stan, it's in pain."

The feral vampire slammed into the door and sent a shock-wave through the room.

"I can repel it," said Andi.

"No! You spend more power, you're going to need to re-place it quicker! You can't risk it!"

"What? You want to just wait until morning?"

"Sit tight," I said. "It's me it wants. I've got a plan."

Okay, so I lied. I didn't have a plan. I didn't even have an idea or a notion. All I had was the thought that I didn't want Andi going crazy again. I ran to the front door of the shop and flooded my dead arm with energy. If I was lucky, I might be able to fend it off for a moment or two.

But then what?

The front door opened without a sound and I peeked through the opening. The cloaked figure stood in the alleyway again. The sickening white vampire sniffed under the door like a rabid dog.

For a split second, I pictured myself bravely leading it away, defeating it even, just like in the movies. Then the creature stopped its sniffing and jerked its head my direction. The pit of my stomach dropped out and I had the sudden cold realization that, not only was my life not a movie, I was damned stupid for acting like it was one.

The figure in the cloak gestured at me, and the creature snarled as it sprang my direction. There was no sense in trying to hold the door shut, so I threw it open and stuck my spirit arm out in front of me. The charge inside the desiccated flesh was enough to blow the skull back on a water buffalo.

I think. I've never been attacked by a water buffalo.

As it closed the distance, I closed my eyes and braced for an impact that never came.

"Looking for something, asshole?"

Andi didn't shout, but her voice echoed though the alley and down the street. It wasn't Andi the vampire that stood at the other door. It was Andi the witch, powerful and angry.

Fear her wrath, hear her roar, cue empowering music.

The creature forgot about me. It turned, growled at Andi, and scrabbled in her direction. It was the distraction I needed.

I hot-footed it toward the figure in the cloak.

I made it to within a yard before the cloak billowed and what I later realized was a foot snapped out and caught me in the throat. I fell to the ground and gasped for air. Andi, for her part, summoned the last bit of energy she had and let loose a bright burst of light. The creature screeched in agony and retreated into the shadows. Its owner snapped the leash and stepped over me on the way out of the alley. As the vampire passed, the odor of sweat and decay, old blood and shit followed in its wake. Had I not been busy trying to get air through my neck, I might've thrown up.

Andi stayed vertical long enough to watch them leave the alley, then fell to the ground in a heap. I scrambled to my feet and to her side.

"Andi? C'mon, wake up... Don't do this to me."

"She needs energy," said Lily from the doorway. She looked drained.

"What did you..?"

"Fed her," she said as she slumped to the floor. "Gave her some of my energy."

"Are you out of your mind?"

Lily smiled.

"Worth it," she drawled before her eyes fluttered shut.

Both were seriously depleted, and both needed an energy transfusion. But only one was likely to eat me if she didn't get food, and the other could be solved with another pulled-pork sandwich.

I put the hand of my withered arm over Andi's hand and shifted my perception. Lily's aura was weak, but still the same as I had seen when we met. Andi's, however, was diseased, brown and black with places just... missing. At the heart, however, was a thin corona of white and blue and pink, the colors I knew her by. The energy of my arm pulsed in time with my heartbeat, and the blue of Andi's aura tried to reach through the sludge to get to it.

I gave the energy stored in my arm a gentle nudge and watched as it became a steady stream into Andi's body. As the energy drained, Andi's eyes fluttered open.

"Is it gone?" she mumbled.

"Yeah," I said. "What were you two thinking?"

"Her idea," said Andi. "She said she didn't want to watch you get mangled. I think she likes you. Is she okay? I didn't take too much, did I?"

"She'll be fine," I said, and hoped I was right. "Let's get her upstairs to the couch."

I sat by the couch with a cool, wet washcloth over Lily's forehead while Andi raided the refrigerator. Everything she picked up, she sniffed, made a face, and put back.

"Damn it," she said. "Nothing smells right. Everything just makes my stomach roll."

"I called Norman and left a message," I said. "He should

be getting back to me soon. We'll figure out a more permanent solution as soon as we can."

"Stan," she said. "I'm sorry."

"You were doing what you thought was right," I replied. "Don't worry about it."

"No," she said. "About Lily. When she gave me her energy, I got a glimpse in her mind. She's a good soul. She's pretty messed up, but she's a good soul. I'm sorry."

"No... problem," said Lily from the couch. Her words were slurred like she was drunk, but it was good to hear her voice again. "Oh, my head."

She made to sit up, then slipped right back down again.

"Why'm I so weak?"

"You need food," I said. "You gave her a lot of your energy. Recovery will happen faster if you eat."

"Bring on the grub," smiled Lily.

There was a knock at the door. Everyone still capable of it tensed.

"Stan, it's me. Open up."

I peeked through the peephole. Detective Norman stood on my landing with a blue duffel in his hand and an annoyed look on his face. I opened the door anyway.

"I can't keep doing this," he said as he walked in. "Too much blood goes missing, my ass gets fired. You, young lady, need to go on a diet."

Andi snatched the bag out of his hand and tore it open.

"There's a zipper, you know," he said.

She blew him a kiss as she pulled one of the units of blood out of the bag and used a pair of scissors to cut the end off. Then she poured the sticky crimson inside into a waiting tumbler.

"You're kidding," said Norman.

"Where are the straws?" Andi opened the pantry and rummaged.

"Cabinet over the toaster oven," I said.

Norman and Lily gawked, first at her, then at me. To be honest, it didn't occur to me that either one of us said anything weird until I played the scene back in my head later.

"There's also, y'know, people food," said Norman as he waved a bag of Chinese take-out.

"Hey!" My voice made everyone jump. "She's still people. It's still Andi. She's not a monster."

Norman held his hands up in surrender, then doled out containers of fried rice and sweet-and-sour chicken.

For a while, the only sound in the apartment was the slightly wet noise of people eating. Lily and I were ravenous, and Norman looked like he never missed a meal. For her part, Andi sat on the kitchen counter with her bloody cocktail. Even Bitsy made an appearance to eat whatever scraps she could wrangle with cuteness and cunning.

"Thank you, guys," I said. "Pretty sure that thing would've torn me to pieces."

"I couldn't let that happen," said Lily between bites.

"What thing?" Norman took a big bite of stir-fry.

"Vampire," I said. "Tortured into being feral."

He stared for a moment, not sure if I was serious or not. When he seemed to accept that I was, he took another bite.

"Well, while you were playing vampire hunter, I was doing some detective work."

"Tell me you got a name," I said.

"Not quite," he said. "I do have something. But you're not going to like it."

"I don't like anything about this. What did you find?"

"The bidder did it through a business account," he said. "And it had to be verified through a board of directors."

"What business?"

"It was a corporation called Evergreen International, LLC."

15

There's a moment in movies in which the hero realizes that the big bad isn't just one guy, but a huge faceless entity with lots of clout and deep pockets. The individual, he can deal with. But groups? The hero usually gets a look on his face like he knows he's just stepped in deep shit.

Kind of like the look I probably wore.

"Corporation?" My appetite gone, I pushed my fried rice away. "Like with money and lawyers and power and stuff? *That* kind of corporation?"

"Yeah," said Norman. "And no one really knows anything about them."

"I can find out!" said Andi. She bounced down from the counter and grabbed her laptop off the table. Before I could say anything, she pushed the power button. Inside, I cringed. On the outside I wore my best poker face ever.

The laptop sputtered pathetically and a weak spark flashed

under the keyboard.

"What the hell?"

"That's weird," I said.

Andi's head snapped toward me. If looks could kill, I would've resembled a burnt matchstick.

"What did you do?" she demanded.

"I didn't know where you were," I stuttered. "I was going to try to find you and I... sort of... phased my spirit arm through it."

For the second time, I closed my eyes and waited for an impact. This one came.

"Asshole!" she shouted as she smacked me in the good arm. "Your stupid spirit arm fried my laptop!"

"You can fix it, right?"

"Maybe," she said, a little calmer. "As long as the hard drive isn't burnt, I can have the motherboard replaced. But until then, my search skills are on hold."

"Lucky for us, then," said Norman. "My search skills are just fine. I got an address. And, surprise, it's here. Downtown, in fact."

"Let's go!" I said as I stood.

"Stan," said Norman. "It's two o'clock in the morning. There's no one there, and you're all beat up and exhausted. You need sleep."

"I don't," said Andi. "Sunrise isn't for about five hours. I

202

can go snoop and be back while you guys nap."

"I don't think that's such a good idea." It wasn't that I didn't trust her. I just didn't know if I could anymore.

"I'm okay." She raised her tumbler in one hand and the duffel in the other. "C'mon. Let me help. I'm sorry for being a jerk. I need to do something to help find Daniel. Please?"

Against my better judgment, I nodded. Andi gulped the last of her disgusting beverage and ran out the door.

"I'm going too," said Norman. "I'll be back here sometime after nine. Eleven, tops. You two get some rest."

He closed the door behind him, and I became acutely aware of how small the apartment was, and how accusing Bitsy's eyes could be. Lily stood by the couch and I by the door. The distance between us was several feet, but it felt both cavernous and minuscule at the same time. My heart pounded as I tried to think of something to say that was neither awkward nor cringe-worthy.

"I should go," said Lily after a moment.

"No," I said. "You need rest and you need to stay safe. You can sleep here."

Lily looked at me over the top of her glasses.

"Oh?"

Heat crept up my neck and flooded into my cheeks and ears. My mouth went dry, and I was pretty sure my tongue grew three sizes so it didn't fit in my mouth anymore. I also became very aware of my hands and where they were.

"I... um... I mean... Dammit."

I hurried across the room and opened the door to the bedroom, then stepped aside.

"Here," I said. "I'll sleep on the couch."

She smiled.

"Thanks," she said. "I really appreciate it."

"No problem." I pulled the bedroom door shut behind her. In my nervousness, it slammed. Bitsy sat on the arm of the couch and glared.

"What?" I whispered. "I'm just being nice."

The cat swished her tail accusingly.

"She's a friend," I whispered. "That's all."

Bitsy blinked.

"Oh, what do you know? You're just a cat."

Bitsy narrowed her eyes and jumped down off the couch, as if I'd offended her.

I laid on the couch and pulled one of Maggie's old throw blankets over my shoulders. It still smelled like her, like love and rosemary and lavender. I buried my face in the folds and breathed her in deep. And as I fell into a quick and deep sleep, I hoped I'd dream of happier times.

I awoke to a cat on my face and a knock at my door.

"Hang on!" I shouted as I pushed Bitsy off. Whoever was on the other side of my door knocked again.

"Hurry up, damn it!" It was Norman.

Garish sunlight assaulted my eyes as I threw the door open. Norman had a black bodybag over his shoulder.

I would be lying if I said a cop with a bodybag was the strangest thing that ever turned up at my door.

"Holy... Get inside before someone sees you!"

"Pretty sure that's a lost cause." He shuffled through the doorway. "I'm pretty sure every morning commuter saw me pull this out of the trunk."

"I can hear you, you know." Andi's muffled voice came from inside the bag.

Norman rolled his eyes and stood the body bag up.

"Hurry up!" shouted Andi. When he pulled the zipper down, she flailed her arms until she was free of the light-proof prison.

"I thought you'd had enough of riding in trunks a long time ago," I said with a smirk.

"Hardy har har," she said.

"What's all the noise..?" Lily froze in the doorway of the bedroom. I could only imagine how the whole thing looked from her point of view. A big bear of a cop, a little witch-vampire-girl in a bodybag, and me with morning-face on. The three of us just stared at her, and she at us. "... about?"

"Um..."

"Never mind," she said with a wave of her hand. "It's too early. I need coffee."

Music to my ears.

Lily rummaged through the kitchen while Andi told us what she'd found out, which wasn't much. The building stood alongside the giant glass castle that was PPG Place, and, as far as she could tell, had only one entrance on each side. There were no windows on the ground floor, and every door was locked. Even her Magick couldn't open the doors, which meant someone had warded them. Whoever was inside knew about Magick, and could sling a few spells of his own.

"If no one else is going to ask, I will." Lily stood in the kitchen with her hands on her hips. "What's with the bodybag?"

"I stayed out too long," said Andi. "Sun came up."

"I was driving by," said Norman. "Scoping the place out. I saw her hiding in a culvert."

"And the bodybag?"

"It was in my trunk," said Norman with a shrug. "I've got a supply of them. Cop stuff."

She shook her head and went back to the cabinets.

"Coffee's ready," she said.

The coffee helped to wake me up, but what I really needed, I realized, was a hot shower. After I made sure Andi was safe in the workroom of the shop, Norman took Lily to her home in the west end to get cleaned up and a fresh change of clothes. I made him promise not to leave her alone.

The hot water beat down on my back like a thousand tiny hammers that banged out the dents and kinks in my muscles, and I reveled in the sensation.

Still, just like every other time my mind had nothing upon which to focus, my thoughts wandered.

Daniel. He needed me. Well, he needed someone, and whether or not I was fit to be his parent, I was still his dad. For everything I knew, everything I could do, I couldn't just pull him out of thin air or will him into my arms. And somewhere, in the back of my mind, something told me I was running out of time. I doubted they wanted to raise him, go through the rumored hell of potty training and teenage years. Whatever their reason, he was in danger.

An idea clicked in my brain and I turned off the shower and grabbed for my towel. Instead of focusing on who had him, maybe I needed to focus on why they had him. What possible reason anyone might have for stealing my baby.

Well, he is the son of an insanely powerful witch and a necromancer.

As I came out of the bathroom, I caught sight of the bed. The blankets were still rumpled, and in the center was the outline of a woman. Lily. I knew the impression was hers, but it caught me off guard.

For just a moment, Maggie was back. She was puttering in the kitchen. I could walk out and wrap my arms around her waist and kiss her cheek and hold her close. For one instant, my old life was back and everything else happened in my imagination while I dozed in the shower.

It lasted for only a second or two, but those moments stretched until I could feel their ache in my bones.

I rushed to dress. The room was too small, and I needed to be somewhere, anywhere else that didn't have so many memories attached to it.

What I needed was someone who could find anything, search everywhere all at once, and come up with an answer quick, and the only person I knew who could was Andi. But she needed her laptop, which I had fried.

I didn't bother brushing out my hair as I slipped my shoes on, grabbed her defunct laptop, and ran out the door.

I often do stupid things that, at the time, make perfect sense. I admit it. Most guys will do the same. If we do something wrong, we try to make amends. The problem is that we use what's commonly referred to as "guy logic." Guy logic takes an idea, makes it seem like the brilliant solution to the big problem, and says "what's the worst that could happen?" Most often, guys who fall victim to guy logic wind up confused and terrified.

"What's this?" Andi stared at the large box in my hand.

"Open it," I said.

She didn't bother to mask her suspicion as she ripped off the paper.

"A new laptop? Where's my old one?"

"Traded it in," I said, my smugness evident in my voice.

"You WHAT?"

Guy logic failed me again. There needed to be a cure.

"But the old one was ruined," I said. "This one's better!"

"How could you?" Her eyes brimmed with rage tears. Part of me knew that, unless I thought of something quickly, I wasn't getting out of the workroom alive.

"I saved the brain!" I blurted as I held my hands up to try to prevent my impending doom.

"How?" She narrowed her eyes at me. I needed to tread lightly.

"The guy at the shop. He swapped out the driver, or hard disk, or whatever it's called. He promised you wouldn't lose any of your stuff." I offered a weak, hopeful smile.

"Did he?" She removed the laptop from the box and plugged it in, then pressed the power button.

The time it took between button-push and actual start was excruciating. I felt like a man waiting for a governor's reprieve as he sat in the electric chair. On one side, a person's hand sat on the switch, on the other another person's hand rested on a silent telephone. And the clock ticked on.

After a moment, Andi typed a few strokes and the screen brightened. She didn't smile, but her features softened a bit.

The proverbial telephone rang. I was granted a temporary reprieve.

"Okay," she said. " It looks like everything's here."

"I'm off the hook?"

"For now," she said. "What do you need?"

"See what you can find out about the Evergreen Corporation," I said. "Start with how long they've been in Pittsburgh, and why we've never heard of them before today. And see if you can find out who's on the board."

"On it," she said. "And Stanley? Thanks, but don't ever do that again. Okay?"

I nodded and backed out of the room. It was still early, and there were too many questions that I needed answered. Every person I knew that had been connected with Evergreen was dead, but there was at least one person who, even if he was dead, might be able to give me a little insight.

Too bad he hated me.

Theaters are curious things. No matter where it is or how old, the actors in them claim they are all haunted. It's superstition and hokum, for the most part. To theater people, a ghost in the theater is considered a sign of "good luck." So a lot of them either invoke a spirit or just make one up. It's all in good fun.

Except when the ghosts are real.

The Pittsburgh Playhouse is a delightful little theater, and it's haunted. Very. By a total of four ghosts and one insufferably arrogant demon. And while they're not really much by way of worry, there's at least one who knows me by name.

"Kevin," I shouted. "Are you here?"

"Where else would I be?" The voice hit me like a cold breeze from behind the center stage curtain. I took a deep breath and steeled myself for what was to come.

From behind the curtain emerged a clown. The fact that he died in his costume with a face full of makeup really pissed him off, but I couldn't be bothered by his clothes. It was that he carried his own head like a football under his arm that freaked me out.

"You look like shit," he said.

"You're one to talk." Kevin didn't really like me in life. I hoped death might have mellowed him out. It didn't. He was the ghost that had scared Bradu into submission, but that was a one-off. For the most part, he wanted nothing to do with me. "I need some information," I said. "About Evergreeen."

"Ah, shit." He said. "Evergreen is dead. Can't that just be the end of it?"

"They took my son," I said. "I need to know why."

"Not here," said Kevin. "Downstairs. My dressing room." He popped out of existence.

"Great."

I hated going to Kevin's dressing room. It was less a usable space and more a disused broom closet, deep in the bowels of the building. But it was Kevin's main hangout, for some reason. I didn't particularly care about the location or how dirty and

212

creepy it was so much as I cared about who his neighbors were, and that I was sure to meet them again.

The two dead actors, I didn't mind so much. They kept to themselves. The ghost with a rotten-melting face liked to sneak up behind folks and scare them half to death, but I was used to him. The one I really didn't want to see was the one people called the Bouncing Red Meanie.

At one time, he'd been a tempter demon, but he got bit by the theater bug. He never left, and every time I ventured into what he considered his theater, he took the opportunity to annoy me.

When I arrived at his dressing room, Kevin was already there, head on his shoulders where it should've been.

"I need you to tell me what you know about the Evergreen Corporation," I said. "Like who's in charge of it and why they would want my son."

"Evergreen was set up by Bill and Brea," he said. "Long time before I met them. I don't know who took it over when they died, but it's a safe bet they're just like Bill and Brea. As for your son, I'm betting they're rebuilding and they need the blood of an innocent to do it."

"Why mine? They killed my mom to get to him. Why go through all the trouble?"

"I don't know," he said. "Spite, maybe? I'm sorry about

your mother. But you're the one who took Evergreen down, so I'm betting they killed her and took him to get back at you. Plain and simple."

"Nope." The voice climbed the back of my neck like spider feet and made my stomach churn. "Wrong again, clown-boy."

I turned. The Bouncing Red Meanie stood in the doorway, a smug grin on his face.

"Hello, Ukobak."

To know a demon's name is to command him, or at least to show a perceived superiority. And, where most demons are concerned, to call one out is to tempt fate.

He hated it when I used his proper name, but he hated his nickname even more.

"Cooper. You don't have any idea what's really going on, do you?"

"Like you do?"

"Of course I do," he said. "Innocent blood's not enough. Your kid's special. He's got half a demon in him, remember? Plus he's the child of both worlds, and add in his mother's power to boot... It's a wonder you don't have every demonic nut-case banging down your door on a daily basis."

Terrible images flashed through my mind, each nastier than the last. The power Daniel held was always a question for me. Sure, it had killed Maggie, but I was never certain just what it could do, how much he really had. If he was as powerful as the demon said, whoever took him might have far worse plans than his death.

"They're drawing more power," I said. "Something called a syphon. They've killed Bob, Reneau and Blossom already."

"Blossom?" Kevin's image faded for a moment. "She's dead?"

"I thought you would know." It really never occurred to me that he wouldn't.

"How the hell would I know that?" Kevin's image swelled, a product of his rage. "It's not like I can sense that kind of shit!"

"I'm sorry," I said. "I guess I just thought you would know somehow. It came for them. It killed Bob in his church, Reneau in her own home. Blossom died protecting her animals."

"Of course she did," said Kevin. His image faded again. "They were her life. They'll be coming for me next, I'll bet."

"What're you talking about? You're already dead."

"He's still so dim, isn't he?" Ukobak shook his head in mockery. "Souls, boy. Energy. A syphon sucks up energy in the form of souls."

"When a ghost gets taken by a syphon," said Kevin, "That's it. It's death for the dead."

The hair on my arm stood up as his meaning took hold. It didn't kill them. It obliterated them. Ended their whole existence.

No moving on, no afterlife, no haunting. Nothing. The syphon finished them. No second chances. Permanent.

"How do I stop it?"

"No clue," said Kevin. He wouldn't meet my eyes, and I had a pretty good idea that, even if he knew, he wouldn't tell me. Kevin hated his existence, and the erasure of his friends could only make it worse.

"What about you?" I turned to the demon. "You know all about this stuff. How do I kill it?"

"How do you kill a puff of smoke?" His red eyes twinkled. "Or stab a cloud? How do you murder a puppet without strings? You don't. The only way for you to stop it is to stop the person holding its leash."

"Can you protect him?" I jerked my head toward Kevin. "From the syphon?"

"Why should I?"

"Because once it finds out you're in here, what's to stop it from sucking you dry too?"

A broad smile crossed Ukobak's face.

"I'd like to see him try," he said. "But I see your point. Don't worry. The thing can't get in here. The whole building is under my protection. Consider it my civic duty as a patron of the arts."

"You're sure?"

"Dear boy, as long as he stays in this building, nothing

short of the Almighty Himself could get to him."

I nodded and turned to leave.

"Cooper." Kevin's voice stopped me. There was so much hate, so much sorrow in two syllables that I couldn't walk away. "Find who did this. Make them pay for killing Blossom. Please."

In life, Kevin never said please to me. Not even once.

"I will," I said.

"Hope you find your kid," said Ukobak. "One Hell's enough for me."

I turned to ask what he meant, but he was gone, and so was Kevin.

As I made my way back out to my car, my cellphone rang.

"Cooper."

There was nothing on the other end of the line but static. For a moment, I thought my service had crapped out again. But then I listened for just a moment longer.

In the background, just beyond the hiss of static, a baby cried.

My baby. My knees buckled and I hit the sidewalk.

"Hello? Who is this?"

"Coming for you." The voice was a whisper, neither male nor female. Just breath formed into words by lips.

"Please," I said. "Don't hurt him."

The line went dead. I sat on the sidewalk and stared at my

217

phone like I expected it to speak again. The call history showed only that someone had called, but didn't tell me who. It didn't even tell me a number, just "unknown."

Coming for you.

He had my phone number. Which meant odds were good he knew where I lived. How long had he watched? Waited? How many opportunities did he have to snatch Daniel before I came back? How many since?

I pushed to my feet and ran to my car. As I ran, I dialed. Andi answered on the second ring.

"Stan," she said. "I found—"

"Are you safe?"

"What?"

"Are. You. Safe?"

"Yeah," she said. "I'm fine. Why?"

"Have Lily and Shannon made it back?"

"Who's Shannon?"

"Detective Norman!" I shouted. "Are they there?"

"No," she said. Panic crept into her voice. "Why? What happened?"

"Sit tight," I said. "I'm on my way. If they get there before me, let them in, close up and tell the shop to lock down."

"You're scaring me," she said. "What the hell's going on?"

"Just do what I asked," I said. "I've got to try to call them."

I hung up and punched in Norman's number. The phone went to voicemail.

"It's me," I said. "When you get this, head to the shop. I need to talk to you."

Lily's number was next. She answered on the first ring.

"Hi, Stan."

"Where are you?" I tried to keep the panic out of my voice, but I failed miserably.

"On my way back to your place," she said. "Why?"

"Hurry," I said. "Get there and get inside and don't leave the shop for anything."

"Okay," she said. "Why?"

"Because the person who took Daniel is coming after me, and I'm betting everyone I care about too. The shop's safe. Now hurry. Andi's waiting for you."

"That doesn't make me feel better," she said.

"Please, just trust me."

"Alright," she said after a pause. "Where are you?"

"Twenty minutes away," I said. "I'll meet you there."

I hung up and got into my car.

17

Twenty minutes turned to fifteen with the blessed aid of good traffic and a serious case of leadfoot. I careened into the parking lot of the shop, and was relieved to see the front windows were solid black. Lily's car sat in the third parking space. That meant the only person missing was Norman, and my gut churned at the thought.

When I came through the back door, I found Lily and Andi on opposite sides of the summoning circle. Each stared at the other intently. I wondered how long they'd been there.

"Am I interrupting?"

"Thank the Goddess," said Andi. She leapt off her barstool and ran to give me a hug. It was something she'd done a thousand times on as many occasions. I tried not to flinch.

"Is everything okay?" Lily stayed on her perch. "Where's Norman?"

"I don't know," I said. "I can't get hold of him."

"The sun'll be down in about an hour," said Andi. "I can feel it. If he's not here by then, I'll go looking for him."

"No," I said. "It's not safe. This new Evergreen is coming for me. I don't want any of you to get hurt."

"I can't stay in," said Andi. "I'm getting hungry again. There's only one blood bag left, and if I'm cooped up in here, I can't guarantee anyone's safety." She said the word "anyone" with emphasis and cut her eyes toward Lily. I got the hint.

"Fine," I said. "But you check in every hour, you got me?"

"Yes sir!" She saluted and slumped back onto her barstool. "I'm a big girl, y'know."

"Yes, and what happened the last time you went out?"

"Like that's going to happen again," she snorted. "They can't turn me twice."

"But you can turn other people," I said. "What'll you do if your hunger gets the best of you and I'm not there to help?"

Andi looked down at her shoes. She knew I was right, even though she hated to admit it. And I hated to see her so down on herself.

"You said you found something out," I said. "What?"

"Yeah." She slid off the barstool and moved to the work counter where her computer, a collection of stickers already present on the new case, sat open. The screen saver busily added afros to the works of Andy Warhol. When she pressed the touch pad, the screen jumped.

"Evergreen," she said. "The oldest records of it I can find in Pittsburgh date back to around 1850."

"So it's been around for a while."

"Well, the weird thing is that I've found mention of the name in the same context as far back as 1582. In Europe. And there are allusions to it going back even further."

"Okay," I said. "So what are they?"

"From what I've been able to find, they were originally keepers of sacred knowledge."

Tumblers of the lock inside my brain turned.

"What do they do now?"

"Looks like commodities," said Andi. "But they're very vague on their website, and I can't find much else out about them."

"Wait... They have a website? Does it list their board of directors?"

"No," she said. "I couldn't find one."

"Keep looking," I said. "Someone has to know who runs the place."

"Who're you looking for?"

"William Keith."

I'll admit, I'm kind of thick sometimes. When confronted

with a puzzle, the pieces don't always fit. Hell, sometimes, I'm not even aware there's a puzzle at all. But when the pieces start to come together, something clicks in my head and the bigger picture becomes clear.

I wasn't there yet, but the picture was getting less hazy.

If I was right, William Keith, affectionately known as Bill-the-psycho-mage-who-tried-to-kill-me, was on the board of directors, along with his wife, Brea. And if I was lucky, Andi might be able to find the name of his successor.

"It's amazing," said Lily. "How much information that kid can sift through so quickly."

Andi sat engrossed, a state I called "nerd-vana," by her computer screen. Her fingers danced across the keyboard and pages flashed by so fast I didn't even have time to read a single word. She was in her element, and it was cyberspace.

"Yeah," I said. "One of her many talents."

Even though we couldn't see the sun outside, we knew when it dipped below the horizon. Andi's demeanor changed. The spell of her computer screen was broken, not an easy feat, and she rose from her stool.

"Find anything?"

"Huh?" Andi stared at the door, eyes wide, expression blank. "No. Yeah. I mean... Maybe. I need to, um..."

"Hey." I got her attention, but made sure to keep a healthy

distance. "You here?"

"Yeah," she said. "Sorry. I'm just... I'm getting antsy. I need to get out of here. I'm not hungry yet. No worries there. Just... I need to get out. Look for Norman."

Her speedy talk and stutter routine reminded me of a conversation I once had with a meth head. She was still in control, though only just. Her tone was one I recognized as the voice of addiction.

"Okay," I said. I motioned Lily to stay behind me. "I get it. You need to go out, but stay close, okay? You don't want to hurt anyone else."

Andi turned fierce eyes toward me.

"What's that supposed to mean?"

"Nothing," I said as I raised my hands. "I didn't mean anything by it, okay? I just want to be where I can help if you need me, okay?"

She nodded and ducked out the back door.

"Wow," said Lily when she was gone. "Some shift."

"You didn't know her before," I said. "She's always been fierce. This new vampire thing, though. I don't know what to do about it."

"You'll get no advice from me," said Lily. "I have no idea what to do or how I would handle it. For what it's worth, though, I think you're doing the best you can."

"Thanks."

We sat in awkward silence for a few moments. There was a lot I wanted to say, but wasn't sure I should, or if I was allowed. I wasn't even sure if what I felt was real or just the product of being lonely.

"Hey," I said after a moment. "You know everything about me, but it just occurred to me. I know next to nothing about you."

"What would you like to know?"

We spent the next hour and a half swapping stories. How she grew up in Texas, how her mom was an English teacher and her father was an attorney. She told me about when her abilities first manifested, and how she, like me, didn't know how to handle them. Unlike me, she didn't have someone to guide her. She'd had to learn to control the visions on her own, and that's when she found art, and figured out how to use it. She was vague about how she wound up in Pittsburgh, but I got the impression that an ex-boyfriend was involved, so I let the subject drop.

She smiled when she talked, a self-deprecating grin that let me know she made mistakes, but she owned them. When anything particularly embarrassing came up, she stared at her shoes. When she laughed, she laughed with her whole body, and when she was sad, everything about it reflected in her movements.

Somehow, we wound up sitting at the workbench on stools,

a little too close to be just friends. I told her the story of what happened to my arm and she didn't flinch when she touched my burnt hand. It was nice, and for a moment I felt, if not happy, then at peace.

The back door opened, then closed as Andi came through the curtain.

"I couldn't find him," she said. "I've looked all over..."

She stopped and stared at us. We drew our hands away from each other as if we were awkward teenagers caught by our parents.

"...the west end," she said, an edge to her voice. "Nothing. Has he called?"

"No," I said.

Lily excused herself to the restroom. When the door shut, Andi shot me a look and gestured for me to follow her through the curtain into the main part of the shop.

"What the hell is going on?"

"What?" My cheeks grew hotter. "Nothing. We're just talking, that's all. Like friends."

"Friends, huh?" She scoffed. "Looked like more than friends to me."

"Will you knock it off? Look, I like her, okay? Is that such a problem for you?"

"But Maggie..."

"Maggie is dead." I wished I could take it back, but it was the truth. "And I can't change that. I will love her for the rest of my life, and nothing will change that either, but I also think she wouldn't want me to be lonely. I don't think she would want me to spend the rest of my life grieving."

"What about Daniel?"

"What about him?"

"Is this person going to be his new mother?"

"Whoa, slow down! You're making a whole bunch of leaps here. Look, I like her, okay? That's where our relationship is right now. We're not in love, we're not getting married, we're not even discussing any of that. We are, for now, just friends, okay? Now can you please give it a rest? I've got enough on my mind without this kind of drama."

"Maybe I should leave." Lily stood in the doorway.

I stood frozen for a moment, unsure of what to say or do.

"No," said Andi. "I should. Look, I'm sorry. I couldn't find Norman and Maggie is... was... very special to me. I just... It's hard, you know?"

"I don't," said Lily. "I've never been through this. But I can imagine. I don't want to replace Maggie. It's obvious you guys loved her very much, and I wouldn't even dream of trying. I wouldn't even know how to begin trying to. But, if you let me, I'd like to be your friend."

Seconds ticked by. I'm not sure I even breathed.

"I think I'd like that," said Andi. "It's going to take time, but I think I'd like that."

"Me too," said Lily.

"I should probably get back out there," said Andi. "There's a lot of night left and I only searched a small part of the city."

"How about you wait for a bit," I said. "I don't like the idea of you being out there when someone's out to hurt the people I care about. Besides, Norman's a cop, right? He's probably fine. He'll probably come banging on the door any second now and..."

My phone rang, number unknown.

I should really learn to keep my big mouth shut.

My stomach flipped and my hands sweated as I pushed the "accept" button. A desert blew through my mouth and throat.

"Hello?"

Silence on the other end of the line for a few seconds.

"Who is this?"

"S... Stan?" The voice was Norman's.

"Shannon?"

"I... I fucked up," he said. "Big time. They got me."

"Who? Where are you?"

"Don't know. Bag over my head. I can't see. It hurts. Stan... It hurts so bad..."

In the background, my son cried. Shannon's voice moved

229

away, and he stifled a sob. I waited.

"One down," the whisperer said. "I'll take them all."

"You son of a bitch... What do you want?"

The phone went dead.

I threw the receiver across the room. It hit the wall and pieces flew off. It was a childish move, but there was nothing else to be done, and I felt so impotent.

"I can track him," said Andi. I spun to face her. "Really. I can track him. I can get his scent and follow him anywhere. This new vampire thing has perks, I'm discovering."

"What do you need?"

"Something he touched or wore."

I couldn't think of anything he left behind. He kept his jacket on hand, always cleaned up after himself. It wasn't like he just left a sock in the bathroom or anything. Then an idea struck.

"How about a place where he sat?"

Andi cut her eyes at me, then let out a heavy sigh.

Upstairs, I gestured to the chair next to the coffee table. Andi glared.

"Not a word about this," she said, then bent down to the seat where Detective Shannon Norman's butt had sat only hours before. She drew in a deep breath through her nose once, twice, then sat up and sniffed the air.

"Did you..?"

"Got him," she said.

I ran back into the shop. Lily stood by the door, her face creased in worry.

"We'll be back," I said. "Stay inside. The shop will protect you."

Lily nodded and put her arms around my neck. She was warm, soft to the touch and for a moment, I forgot why I was leaving. She kissed my cheek.

"Be careful," she said.

"Please, keep her safe," I said to the shop. "I... She means a lot to me."

Before Lily could respond, I ducked out the door. It bolted shut behind me as I hurried to the car.

18

Too many people I loved were dead. Too many were lost in the insane metaphysical world that I found myself thrust into when I died and came back. Maggie. Mom. Taylor. Appel. Some friends. Some acquaintances. A whole lot of strangers. None of them deserved it. None of them would have died, should have died, but they had the unfortunate commonality of coming into contact with me. Blossom. Kevin. Reneau. Neighbor Bob. A body count of impressive proportions by any standard. And it all led back to me. I lost my arm. Andi lost her humanity. And Norman...

Norman wasn't lost yet.

I drove through the nighttime traffic at breakneck pace and followed wherever Andi's inhuman nose took us. The closer we got to the center of downtown, the worse the feeling in my gut got. Every turn brought us closer to a place I never wanted to see again. Deep down, however, I knew before we left where we would end up.

While Bill and Brea were alive, they owned a warehouse on Brunot Island in the Ohio River, just down from the West End Bridge. A lifetime of flim-flammery and carnival gear gathered dust within its walls. It was also a place where Bill liked to hide things. And people.

We drove past the power station and parked outside the security gate. Andi was out of the car before I could stop her and crept to the gate like a predator.

"He's here," she said. "I can smell him."

"Tracked by butt-sweat," I said.

"It worked, didn't it?" She sniffed the air. "Stan... I smell blood."

The gate stood open and the guard was nowhere to be seen, both bad signs.

Andi dashed ahead, from shadow to shadow like liquid darkness. It was unnerving, the speed and grace with which she moved. Part of me wanted to keep her in my heart and mind as Andi, the spunky, punky cyber-witch with mad search skills and questionable fashion sense. But as she darted about, I saw a side of her I didn't like, a side that frightened me.

When we got to the right unit, she froze.

"I can't go in there," she said.

"Relax," I said. "I'll help keep you in check."

"No," she grunted. "I mean I can't physically can't go in there. Something is keeping me out."

When I had raided the warehouse before, boobytraps were everywhere. Nasty little psychological snares and fear pits dotted the inside, each more powerful than the one before it, to keep people out, or to make the ones who got in regret their decision. I had disabled them the last time I was in the building. I didn't think to check if they'd been reset.

I shifted my perception, took a deep breath and lowered the carefully built walls in my mind. When I opened my eyes again, I had the strong urge to run.

Around the outside of the warehouse pulsed a shell of energy so dark it was almost opaque. When I approached, it split and allowed me passage, but it rebuffed Andi with angry prejudice. Every time she took a step forward, I swear, I heard it growl. Whatever was inside was for me and me alone.

"I got this," I said. "Be ready if we need to run."

"Hope you brought a gun or something."

I stared at her. I didn't own a gun. Never did. In fact, I wasn't really sure what I would do with one if someone gave one to me. But she had a valid point. In my anger, I had forgotten to take any kind of weapon at all. No salt, no silver, nothing. All I had on me was my wits, my sparkling personality, and the pentacle that hung around my neck. I hoped they'd be enough.

I took a deep breath as I stepped through the opening, then felt it sucked away as the shield closed behind me. I was alone, cut off from anyone and everything that could help me. Whoever it was, he had me right where he wanted me. If he wanted me dead, it was his best chance.

Relics of a time gone by sat draped in a fine coat of dust and shadow, forgotten by almost everyone. The booths triggered memories that weren't mine, of popped balloons and prizes won, sugars spun and peanuts roasted. For a moment, the faint ghost of a calliope drifted through my head. A younger, much more haughty Bill Keith looked down from faded banners while a youthful Brea looked on from others. My footsteps echoed from wooden stall to metal bar, then were smothered by heavy muslin and velvet curtains.

"Norman?" I called. No sense in being quiet. If the killer was about, chances were he knew not only that I'd arrived, but exactly where I was. Besides, I preferred a straight fight to all the sneaking-around garbage.

I left my perception shifted in the hope that any traps the whisperer had laid would be obvious. But the room seemed almost clean. A healthy pack of scats ran between the old trailers and booths, and little specks of dark energy flitted about, but there were no traps that I could find. But there was what appeared to be a beacon. It was faded, weak, but I recognized its pulse, the mix of colors.

"Norman!"

I ran between trailers and around corners until, at the center of the maze created by Bill's lifetime of lies, I found him. Detective Shannon Norman. He'd been hung upside down by shackles clamped to his ankles. His wrists were done up the same way behind his back. Across his eyes was a bloody blindfold and he'd been gagged. A pool of blood gathered below his head.

"Nonononono..."

I ran to his side. Shannon's face was unrecognizable, a mess of cuts and bruises that spoke of the sadistic glee his captor took at his agony. Blood from shallow cuts in his scalp slicked his hair, and more from cuts in his chest ran down his neck and into his nose. He choked and thrashed, but he was too weak.

Even with one arm, I managed to get him down. The shackles were a magician's prop, with hinges that were dummied to move, if one knew how. Once I figured out how to work the winch mechanism, I lowered him to the ground as gently as I could and pulled off the blindfold and the gag. He had broken blood vessels in both eyes.

"Who was it?" I said as I cradled his head. "C'mon, man, who did this to you?"

"Don't know," he croaked. "Never saw."

For a second I thought he died. But his chest moved. It

237

wasn't in a decent rhythm or anything, but he breathed. I'd be happy for small victories. The next big task was to get him out to the car and to Mercy.

I managed to drag him out. It wasn't easy, Shannon was a great deal bigger than me, but I didn't give up and after nearly ten minutes during which time I strained and pulled, I finally got the big galoot outside.

Which, in reality, might not have been a good thing.

Andi crouched outside the door, ready to pounce on whatever came out. When I came through first, her expression softened into relief. When I dragged Norman out behind me, it changed to hunger.

"He's bleeding," she said. There was a strange, empty tone to her voice that I didn't like.

"Yeah," I said. "Bad guy messed him up pretty bad. He's dying."

"That's a shame," said Andi. She crept closer, eyes on the crimson rivulets that fell from his face.

"We have to get him to Mercy!" She didn't seem to hear me. "ANDREA BEDFORD!"

She snapped her eyes to mine, as if only just aware of my presence.

"Right. Yeah!" She stood up and marched over, then took hold of Norman's jacket and heaved.

Between the two of us, mostly her, we got Norman back to the car and shoved him into the back seat. The fast ride to the hospital was tense, to say the least. Andi twitched, shifted, and fidgeted as she tried really hard to not look at the bleeding mess in the back seat. Every now and again, I caught her as she stared at him in the vanity mirror, but she stayed focused.

When we pulled up in the emergency room entrance, she helped me get him to a wheelchair and into triage. It amazed me that I could just say "this man is a cop" and everyone jumped to their feet. Andi waited outside.

"I'm not welcome," she said as she stared at the doors. "Your friend, the caretaker, is keeping me out. I'll wait for you."

Once I was sure Shannon was in good hands, I high-tailed it over to the chapel.

"Barney?"

The old maybe-angel appeared.

"Sorry," he said. "Can't risk letting her in. Too big a risk."

"Whatever," I said. "Look, keep an eye on that one, okay? I don't want to lose anyone else."

"I have a feeling he'll pull through," said Barney with a wink. Then he faded away.

As I crossed back through the emergency room, I passed Shannon's stall on the way out.

"Stan." His voice was weak, but I was glad to hear it.

"Hey! You're going to be okay," I said.

"Shut up," he hissed. "Knew you would come for me."

"Of course you did," I said. "You're my friend. I..."

"No, stupid. He knew. You spent too much time..."

My stomach dropped again.

There's another terrible moment in movies where the hero realizes he's been duped and has made a big, predictable, asinine mistake. It's so common that I look for it when I watch action flicks or thrillers. And when I find it, I laugh that the character was so stupid as to fall for such a ridiculously obvious scheme.

But as I sped through Pittsburgh traffic again, I couldn't help feeling like more of a chump than all of those action icons put together. He killed my mom, demonstrated his will to murder, so why didn't he kill Norman? Simple. He wanted me out of the way so he could do something. And the only target I could think of was hiding in what I thought was a safe place.

The shop's front windows were smashed, broken inward by some unstoppable force. The door, which was supposed to open inward, hung at a lazy angle pointed outward. There were no lights on, no sign of anyone else. Andi didn't wait for the car to stop before she was out and running up the walk to the door.

I pulled up on to the curb and hurried after her. When I

got inside, Andi sat in the middle of the showroom floor in tears.

"She's dying," she sobbed. "Her light's so weak."

I shifted my vision so I could see what she meant. Since the day Andi brought the building to life, the walls glowed bright, pulsed with energy and intelligence. But the pulse was almost non-existent, the light dim. And even though part of me thought such a feeling for a building was ridiculous, I felt a stab of grief.

It was a building, a construct. That it came to life was an accident. But it... no, she was so much a part of our lives. She was our home, our shop. She was like a child to Andi, and I always kind of thought of her as my niece. I couldn't bear the thought of losing her. Would the building crumble the same way a body rotted? She was alive, but did she have a soul? Did buildings have an afterlife?

And if she did die, what then?

I ran to the back of the shop to check the storeroom. Lily was gone. The stools were tipped over, a few other things broken, but robbery wasn't the motive. They took her. They took her to get to me.

My cell phone rang.

"What?"

"Do I have your attention now, Mister Cooper?" He didn't bother to whisper anymore. It was a man's voice. Not someone I recognized, but it was deep, rich. He sounded almost friendly.

241

"What do you want?"

"You know what I want," he said. "I want you to suffer."

Of course he did. I dismantled Evergreen. I killed the two main players. I screwed up their plans for world control.

"That's what this is about, isn't it? That's what it's always been about."

"Of course," he said.

"Fine," I said. "Take me. I don't even care anymore. Just don't hurt them. Please."

"I'll take you when I'm ready," he said. "When I feel you've suffered enough. When you've lost everything you ever loved. Then I'll take you."

My mind raced. There had to be something, some way to bargain for their lives. I was as good as dead, but I couldn't let him kill my son. I couldn't let him kill Lily.

"Wait!" I said. "What about a trade?"

"What're you doing?" whispered Andi.

"I have something you want," I said. "And I'll trade it for the lives of Lily and Daniel."

"What could you possibly have that I would want?" The voice chuckled.

"The book."

I didn't need to tell him what book. The book. The damned tome bound in human flesh and inked in blood. Ever since pages from it had shown up in my mailbox without a postmark, the thing had been nothing but a pain in my ass. So much dark power lay within its pages that I hid it.

There was a pause on the other end of the line.

"You know where it is?" said the voice.

"I do," I said. "And I'll trade it for their lives. You can still have me. But you have to let them go."

Another pause.

"We have a deal," he said. "You know where I am. You have until tomorrow. Do not disappoint me, Mister Cooper."

The line went dead.

"You can't," said Andi.

"He'll kill them."

"But you can't."

"I have to."

"But—"

"What fucking choice do I have?" I didn't mean to shout, but I couldn't stop. "He's going to kill them if I don't give it to him!"

"He'll kill them anyway."

"I know." I slumped to the floor. "How's the shop?"

"Dying," she said.

"It must've been the syphon. Why leave her like this? Why didn't it take everything?"

243

"Maybe it couldn't," she said.

"We have to save her."

"How?"

I didn't have a clue. The only thing I knew was I was tired of losing my friends, tired of death. Tired of feeling like an impotent piece of garbage because all I could do was stand around with my thumb up my butt while sinister outside forces dictated the direction of my life. I pushed myself up off the floor.

"You are the most powerful witch I've ever met," I said. "We are in a living shop dedicated to that energy. Hell, you brought her to life in the first place! There has to be something we can do!"

"Maggie would know," she said.

"Well Maggie's not here, okay? She's fucking dead, okay? And it's my fault she died!"

I don't know why I said it. I don't even know where the sentiment came from. And it wouldn't stop.

"I'm the one who got her pregnant! Me! It was my fault the demon went from me into the baby! She's dead because of me! And everyone else who's died! My fault! My..."

Angry tears ran down my face as my legs went weak and left me on my knees in Maggie's summoning circle.

"Taylor," I said quietly. "Appel. Blossom. Kevin. Reneau. They're all dead because of me. And Maggie. It's my fault. And now the shop's dying, and that's my fault too."

The slap across my face was hard, unexpected, and the sting jarred me out of my self-pity. I looked up into Andi's tear-swollen eyes.

"Don't you dare," she growled. "Don't you dare dishonor her memory like that. Any of their memories! None of it's your fault. You didn't ask for any of it. You didn't kill anyone. Now get up."

"Andi, I—"

"Get. UP!" She grabbed me by the arm and hoisted me to my feet with surprising strength. "Maggie wouldn't want you to give up, and Daniel needs you. He needs his father. Feel like shit later if you have to, but we don't have time for a pity party right now. I need your help."

"What can I do?"

"She's alive because of energy, right?" I nodded. "So she needs another jolt of energy to stay alive, right?"

It made sense, but I couldn't fathom where we' could find another energy source powerful enough.

"Where are the breakers?"

My heart skipped. It couldn't be that easy.

"What're you going to do, use the city's electric grid to put her on life support?"

"Exactly," she said. "Now where are the breakers?"

I used to love basements. To me, they were one of the many perks of living in the northern half of the United States. In fact, when I found out other states didn't have basements, I wondered how the folks who lived there survived. Where'd they store their stuff, or have home offices, or band practice? To me, the thought of not having a basement was downright un-American.

But then the rats came. Not the regular, run-of-the-mill rodents, but people possessed by demonic rats. They used the sewers to pick the city apart, and broke into buildings through their basements. Including the shop's.

Except that was before she'd been brought to life. After Andi accidentally animated her, there wasn't much need to relive the nightmares in the basement. She didn't need city power anymore. She fed off mice and the good feelings and will of everyone who entered. We had shut the breakers off a long time ago to cut down the electricity bill, and it was fantastic.

Always the perfect temperature. Lights at just the right level. Even windows that shaded themselves.

Everyone should have a living building.

I pulled the boards away from the basement door with a pry-bar and stared into the darkness. The rational part of my mind knew there was nothing down there. The hole got patched a long time ago, and Maggie sealed it rock solid. But there were memories in the basement, and they were worse than the real thing any day.

"Want me to see if she's got enough power for light?"

"No," I said. "Let her save her strength. We don't know if this'll work yet."

I didn't trigger my Sight because I didn't want to see the echoes of what happened down there. Instead, I took a flashlight down with me.

The inside of the room smelled. Not the normal musty scent of a basement, but the scent of decay, of putrid bile.

"What the hell..?" I covered my mouth and gagged. "What's down here?"

I turned in place to try to find the source of the stench. When the light hit Andi, my stomach fluttered. In the garish beam of the flashlight, her chalky skin and sunken eyes stood out, not to mention her new forehead brand. She looked both beautiful and terrifying.

"Think about it," said Andi. "If she's alive, there has to be a place for waste."

"The garbage bin?"

"Not quite."

It took me a few beats to figure out what she meant, and when it finally clicked in my head, it was all I could do to not vomit on the floor.

"We need to hurry up and get out of here," I said.

When I located the breaker box, it was as I remembered it. All the breakers were turned off as a subversive middle finger to Duquesne Light and Power.

"Go upstairs," I said. "Yell if there's any change when I flip the switches."

Andi nodded and bounded up the stairs. When she was gone, I looked around the room to no one in particular, but I hoped the shop knew I was talking to her.

"This'll work, right?" I said. "I mean, you'll be okay, right? I hope so. Geez, it just occurred to me that you don't even have a name, do you? Poor girl. Get through this, and I'll try to talk your mama into giving you a name, okay?"

A slight tremor ran through the floor. I hoped it was a yes.

There were seven switches and the main. Each switch fed part of the building, but the main killed them all. I turned on each switch, then stared at the last one.

"Ready?" I shouted.

"Ready!"

"Please be alright." I flipped the switch.

For the space of a breath, nothing happened. For that one agonizing moment, my heart sank because I just knew it hadn't worked.

"Stan!" Andi ran to the top of the stairs. "Stan! Get up

here! You have to see!"

I ran up the stairs as fast as I could. When I got to the workroom, it was fully lit. A gentle breeze blew through the shop again, and the lights pulsed with Pittsburgh power.

"She's okay!" she said. Bloody tears brimmed her eyes. "She's going to be okay!"

"It's a temporary measure," I said. "Until we can figure out how to help her for good, right?"

Andi nodded.

"And she needs a name."

Andi turned to reply, but the bulbs in the workroom flared and shattered. The air went cool.

"She doesn't know how to handle external power," said Andi. "Something's wrong."

I switched my vision.

"Yeah," I said. "And I know what."

19

William Shakespeare once wrote, "When sorrows come, they come not in single spies, but in battalions." It's a clever flowery speech, but my father said it better. He always said, "When it rains, it pours." Pressed for meaning, he shrugged and replied that enemies didn't wait for a good time. They usually all dog-piled on us at once. Just to make life more interesting.

As if my life weren't interesting enough.

The shop hummed and the scent of burning wire filled the air. From outside, something howled.

"Calm her down," I said. "She's going to burn herself out if she keeps this up."

Andi sniffed the air.

"It's the God damned vampire again."

"This needs to stop," I said. "For good."

Waves of energy and heat flew off the shop's walls as she attempted to protect us. But there was too much power. And the more she threw off, the more she threatened to burn out her freshly-connected electric nervous system.

"Calm down!" I shouted. "I'm going to deal with this."

I sounded brave, confident, maybe even a little tough. But the truth was I was too tired and angry to be scared.

"Go out the front," I said. "Try to get around behind them."

Andi nodded as I pocketed a large bag of salt and went to the back door. It didn't take a genius to see who was responsible, but we didn't have time to deal with the problem.

"I'm coming out!"

The alley was cold, and the lamp over the parking lot cast eerie shadows over the whole scene. The person in the long cloak stood at the mouth of the alley with her pale beast on the chain. It strained to get at me, but she didn't let go. Not yet.

"If you're going to kill me, get on with it," I yelled. "I've got shit to do. Otherwise, piss off."

There was a very short list of who the vampire's handler could've been. And I was a little embarrassed it took me so long to figure out who it was. It came down to motive. Who wanted me gone? Who wanted me to not poke around? And who would benefit from real vampire attacks at the vampire club? Only one person I could think of fit the bill.

Cassiopeia lowered her hood and glared at me.

"What's this about now, huh? The broken window? Bill

me. I've got more important things on my mind."

"Your friend wasn't supposed to live," she said.

"So you're hoping that by causing a little vampire problem you can get Nocturnity shut down and then you'll have the club all to yourself, right? You're such a pathetic bitch."

She let go of the chain and the pasty monster at the end snarled and made slow, deliberate movements toward me. I forced all the energy I could muster into my withered arm. If it wanted a fight, it would get one.

The vampire broke into a run and I threw my withered arm between us with all my energies raised in a Hail-Mary shield. I didn't have nearly the raw animal strength it did, but all I needed to do was buy some time. Just a few seconds.

It slammed into me with about the same amount of force as a runaway truck and knocked me against the wall. It was all I could do to keep on my feet with my arm between us as it pressed into me and snapped its teeth.

They weren't like the movies showed, with two long fangs on the top and two on the bottom. His mouth looked like a bear trap with razorwire in place of the jagged metal clamp. As it snapped, I realized there would be far more damage than just two holes, and the tears in Andi's skin meant she either fought him off better than I could, or she got really lucky.

Ego dictated the latter.

I pushed back as hard as I could, braced my foot against the wall, and tried to leverage a little more strength. But I couldn't hold it. The vampire kept coming. I wasn't sure if he would eat me or crush me. Or both.

In the corner of my vision, Cassiopeia watched me fight with dispassionate indifference. My death wouldn't matter to her any more than any of the others did.

Something dark dropped from above her, and by the time she noticed, it was too late. Andi pounced.

When its master screamed, the vampire's head snapped around, and it let me go. It gave me a split second, just enough time to do a little mojo of my own. Of course, I didn't know if it would work, but it was worth a try.

The creature screamed as a handful of salt flew into its face, and little puffs of smoke came up wherever a grain touched. As it clawed at its eyes, I took the advantage and ducked under its arm and used my shoulder to ram it into a corner, then I poured a line of salt in front of it so it couldn't get out. A little triangle prison, made just for the big pale nasty monster. Then I hurried over before Andi ate the bad guy.

She crouched over Cassiopeia's cowering form, face inches away, teeth bared. The energies around her flickered from what I used to know as her colors to great swaths of red with black at the tips. I switched my vision back because I couldn't stand to see her so transformed.

"You bitch," she said, her voice low and menacing. "Take a good look at what you did to me. I'm going to suck every last drop of blood from your marrow…"

"Andi?"

She snapped her head toward me and snarled. The pupils of her eyes were so dilated that her whole eye looked black. And there were those teeth, jagged and terrifying. They hadn't looked like that moments ago, but she looked every bit the predator as she bore down on Cassiopeia.

"Please," she cried. "Don't kill me! I'm—"

"Remember how I begged?" growled Andi. "Remember how every one of your victims begged for their lives before you turned your pet loose on them?"

"Andi."

"She deserves to die," said Andi. She didn't bother to look at me as she spoke. "Slow and painful."

"You're better than that," I said.

"Am I?" She gave a wicked smile and leered. "I used to be, until she made me into this thing! What're you going to do? Call the police? Tell them she's guilty of assault with a vampire? She'll be out in an hour."

She had a point, and I couldn't argue. But I still didn't want her to become like the walking nightmare that stood watching in the corner of the alley. Not my Andi. It would be worse than if she'd died because not only would I lose her, I'd also have to hunt her.

"You can't kill her," I said. "It's not who you are."

Andi's eyes met mine. Bloody tears streaked her face. There was more than rage in her eyes. They were full of frustration and despair. But also acceptance. She knew I was right.

"You got lucky," she said. She pushed herself off the simpering woman on the ground. Andi hoisted Cassiopeia to her feet and slammed her against another wall.

"How did you control him?" I needed to know. There was a plan forming in my head, and I needed a few ingredients before it could flower.

"I'm not telling you," she sneered.

Andi slammed her against another wall.

"Tell me, or I'll let her do what she really wants to do."

Cassiopeia stared at Andi then reached into her cloak. When she pulled her hand out again, she held her secret.

It was beautiful in its simplicity, a single glass vial wrapped in a basket of silver wire. The vial was filled with thick, dark red.

"This, okay? The blood's his. From before he was like this. When he still had his mind. Silver wire keeps him in check."

"It's sympathetic Magick," said Andi.

"Give it over," I said.

"He hates me," said Cassiopeia. "If you take that away from me, he'll tear me apart."

"You deserve it!" snarled Andi. "I can feel his pain! He's your slave! Why?"

"Those freaks took over the club! They were cutting into my customers."

"Money?" Andi pressed hard against Cassiopeia's throat. "You did this all because of money? You greedy bitch!"

I glanced both ways down the alley. It was a wonder no cops were on the scene yet. The vampire crouched in the corner, his head cocked as if he listened to our conversation. I didn't know if he understood us or not, but I wasn't taking any chances.

"Gimme," I said as I snatched the charm from Cassiopeia's hand. The creature flinched. I approached the beast with caution, charm held up so he could see it.

"This," I said. "Is this how she kept you in line?"

The creature snarled.

"I'll give it back," I said. "But I need to know you won't go trying to kill me or my friends, and I need you to do something for me first."

I'm not a fan of vigilante justice. I mean, I like Batman as much as the next nerdy guy, but that's a comic book. In real life, a guy dresses up like a flying rat, chances are there are more than a few screws loose in his brainpan. Once a person starts taking the law into his or her own hands, society crumbles. To tell the truth, I just don't want someone else's ambiguous rules dictating how I have to behave. That's why we have police, so that everyone has the same set of rules, and no one is above the law. Break the law, go to jail. It should be as simple as that.

But then, there are gray areas in which the law doesn't like to play.

Case in point: Cassiopeia made terroristic threats. Crime. She was directly responsible for the deaths of more than a dozen people. Crime. She used a feral vampire as her murder weapon.

The police van screeches to a halt and the cops driving suddenly become deaf, mute, and blind. They see nothing, hear nothing, and for damned sure aren't going to say anything about any vampires. Which leads to a conundrum.

What to do with the bad guy.

It was still dark, way past what a normal club would call closing time. Nocturnity, however, still had its doors open. There was little traffic. The only people inside were Ravenwood's friends, or maybe a few diehard vampire wannabes. But the throng of crushed velvet and plastic fangs was nowhere to be seen.

I walked through the door, past the doorperson, with Andi by my side and Cassiopeia in tow. Ravenwood sat at the bar with a drink in his hand, his expression miserable.

"Whadda you want?" he slurred.

"I brought you a present," I said. "You want to know who's been sabotaging your club? It's your business partner."

"Cass?" He staggered off his bar stool. "What the hell is he talking about?"

She wouldn't look at him, much less answer. So I did it for her, and I wasn't gentle about it.

"She's the one who killed your patrons."

"Bullshit," he said. "How? Police said they were killed by a wild animal."

"Yeah," I said. "About that."

I whistled. The vampire dropped from wherever it hid on the ceiling and landed in the middle of the dance floor. What few patrons were around screamed and ran out the door. Ravenwood was too drunk to flinch.

"Really?" he said. "A real vampire? You cunt." He made to swing at her, but missed and wound up on his face on the floor.

"I gave her a choice," I said. "Either turn herself in to the police and confess to every murder, or she could face him." I nodded toward the vampire. "She chose the latter. Figured, since you're into this whole vampire thing and it's your club, you'd want to watch."

"What?"

"You keep playing vampire," I said. "I thought you might

259

want to see what a real one looked like."

"I don't..."

"They're not all velvet capes and shitty accents," I said. "Vampires are death, plain and simple."

I backed away from Cassiopeia and the vampire crouched. It sprang as I made my way out the door with Andi in tow. No matter how mad I was, no matter how many heinous acts she'd committed, I couldn't just stand there and watch the creature maul her.

Truth be told, I thought she'd take prison.

Andi and I stood outside by the door until the screaming stopped. It only took a few minutes, maybe even seconds, then the door flew open and Ravenwood stumbled out onto the side-walk and vomited into the gutter.

"Still wanna play vampire?" Andi gave him her cruelest smile.

"It wasn't his fault," I said. "This whole situation sucks." It didn't matter that Cassiopeia chose her end. That I was the one who made her make the choice chewed at me from the inside.

20

I'm not a hero. I don't wear a cape, and I would probably look awful in tights. More, though, the responsibility would smother me. People look up to heroes as an ideal, a symbol of things that are good and just. I can't be that. I'm just a guy, with flaws and bad habits, just like everyone else.

Every now and again, however, I think of how nice it must be to have people look at you with adoration, to get to ride off into the sunset. To get the girl.

Andi had to wait in the back of the shop. It was for the best, seeing as she couldn't cross the threshold to my building anyway. And, if she did manage to make it past the front door of the building, the door to my apartment was so heavily warded that I wasn't sure a simple invitation would keep her from being turned to ash.

Not that it mattered. I didn't want her in my apartment anyway. Not because it was my territory, but because I didn't want her to know what I kept there.

She knew a few things, like the book and a dozen or so haunted baubles. But if she knew how the collection had grown, she would probably be appalled. Also, there was that whole thing with plausible deniability. If she didn't know something was in my vault, she wouldn't have to lie if asked. And people did ask.

I also didn't want her in my apartment because of the danger. Sure, the wards kept nasties out, but it also kept at least a few of the horrors I collected in. For example, a real nasty piece of work that I picked up a while ago was a doll. It didn't look like much, kind of like a monkey in a sailor suit. The thing was old enough it should've been in a museum. But living creatures don't get put in museums, and the ones who torture children and murder adults usually get burnt. Except he didn't burn. Whatever Magick had brought him to life wanted to make sure he stayed that way. So I took him, locked him in my vault, and hoped he'd never get out. And, of course, he did. Every chance he got. I never actually saw him move, but he was always in a different place whenever I came back to the apartment. I kind of considered the place his, after a while.

The door opened with a light creak, and I flipped the light switch.

The damned doll sat on the couch.

"Oh good," I said. "You're up. Don't mind me. Won't be but

a second."

I hurried through and entered the spare bedroom that I called The Vault. Every hair on my skin prickled as I walked through the doorway, all the dark energy washed over me. Every object in the room jockeyed for position on my soul, tried hard to corrupt me, to tempt me, wanted out to do more harm to the world. My mind was awash with offers of every kind from the entities in that room. But I didn't have time for them. I needed the book if I were to save Daniel. And Lily.

The incantation Maggie taught me for disabling the wards was simple, and the words weren't really as important as the will and intent. One thing I had learned from experience, however, was that touching the damned thing was more dangerous for me than for the average person, which was why I had a pair of oven mitts in my bag. I put them on and pulled the book off its resting place, then closed the door behind me as I exited the vault.

As I turned to face the rest of the room, I noticed the doll was no longer on the couch. It stood in front of the door.

"I need it," I said. "For Daniel and Lily." That I felt the need to explain myself to a doll didn't seem odd at all. But it didn't budge, and the thought of touching it set off all kinds of danger warnings in my head. I backed up and sat on the couch.

"You don't understand," I said. "He's my son, and that son of a bitch is going to do something horrible to him. I know it.

And Lily... I like her."

It still didn't move. Just sat there and stared at me with those judgmental beady black button eyes.

"You know something? It just occurred to me that I never knew what your name was. Everyone I know of just called you 'that damned doll.' Can I give you a name?"

It stared back.

"I'm going to call you Owen. Seems stupid for me to call you 'doll' all the time. What do you think? Owen?"

It may have been my imagination, but it seemed like the doll's expression softened just a fraction.

Then I got an idea. A crazy, stupid, wonderful idea.

"Owen, I think maybe I may have a job for you. You think you might be interested?"

The doll's black eyes twinkled.

It took me twenty minutes to get back across the bridge to Carson Street. A police car sat on the curb in front of the shop. In our meager parking lot, the brown piece-of-shit land-yacht that Menold drove took up both parking spaces. Bad vibes filled the air.

I circled the block until I found a space, then made my way to the shop. I went through the front door and into a heated argument, already in progress.

"I don't have to tell you shit!" Andi needed to learn how to control her temper. "Unless you have a warrant, you can get the hell out of my shop!"

"I'm just trying to find him, okay?" Menold sounded tired. Not even angry, just worn out. "He's not in any real trouble, but I've got questions for him, okay? Now where is he?"

I stashed my backpack beneath the front counter and hurried to the back to see if I could keep Andi from being dragged out into the sunlight and off to jail.

"Something I can do to help?" I tried to appear as non-threatening as possible. The look on Menold's face let me know that I looked like death warmed over, most likely due to lack of sleep. Also, I needed to eat again.

"Stanley Irving Cooper!" shouted the young uniformed policeman. "You are under arrest for..."

"Calm down, Slick." Menold put his arm out between the uniform and me. "We're not arresting anyone just yet."

The uniform looked genuinely disappointed.

"Stan, did you go by the nightclub named Nocturnity last night?"

"Yes."

"And when you went, was there a woman with you named Cassiopeia Lynn?"

"I didn't know Lynn was her last name, but yes, there was."

Menold took a deep breath, squeezed his eyes shut, and pinched the bridge of his nose.

"Cassiopeia Lynn was found this morning in a parking lot about four blocks from the club. Coroner says she'd been torn apart by a wild animal, and he places her time of death at around 4 a.m. Witnesses state they saw you in the club with her. Do you have any idea what happened to her?"

"Vampire attack."

I'm not sure why I said it.

Maybe it was one of those moments where I thought the truth would be too ridiculous to be believed. Maybe I thought Menold would shake his head and walk away. Maybe I was punchy from lack of sleep. Whatever the reason, once it was out of my mouth, I couldn't stifle the stupid grin that came along with it. In fact, I couldn't even wipe it away while the other cop slapped the handcuffs on and put me in the back of his cruiser.

There was a point in my life that the thought of going to jail terrified me. My head was filled with images of poorly lit cells and guys with names with a "the" in them, like Izzy the Nose and Harry the Toucan, and all-too-vivid images of why not to drop the soap in the shower.

Live and learn, I guess.

I sat on the metal bunk in the holding cell. Bastards took

my shoe laces, my belt, anything I could've used to cause myself harm. It was odd that I was the only one in the cell. Pittsburgh had a vibrant criminal subculture, but most of it dealt with car-jackings and the occasional domestic squabble. Still, it was nice to have the cell all to myself for once.

Officer Menold was kind enough to keep me updated on Norman's condition. He was on the mend, out of the woods, so to speak, but he couldn't stop shaking. I knew the feeling.

Twenty-four hours. That's all the whispering son of a bitch gave me to get my son and Lily back. And the clock on the wall wouldn't make up its mind. If I didn't watch, it leapt ahead. If I did, it crawled. Either way, every hour that passed meant the window for getting them back got more and more narrow.

I had a plan. I had everything I needed. The only thing I lacked was freedom, and the intelligence to keep my wise mouth shut.

"How long are you guys going to hold me?"

Menold shrugged.

"Legally, we can detain you for twenty-four hours without cause."

"I have to get out of here," I said. Panic crept into my voice. "In twenty-four hours, the guy who has my kid is going to kill a girl and keep my kid for good."

"Who?" Menold stood with his arms crossed in front of

the cell door like an angry principal.

"I don't know his name," I said. "But I know where he is. The building next to PPG Place downtown."

"Fine," said Menold. "You should've told us immediately. I'll send a squad car down and..."

"You'll get them killed," I said. "It has to be me."

Menold glared, his face unreadable.

"C'mon, Mark," I said. "You know me. I'm weird, but I'm not a liar, okay?"

"Fine. Tell me what happened to Cassiopeia."

"You wouldn't believe me if I told you," I said.

"Try me."

I let out a long sigh. I learned a long time ago that, as far as police were concerned, the whole "try me" tactic never worked. No matter what I said, he wouldn't believe a word of it.

"Cassiopeia Lynn was the one responsible for about half of your missing persons," I said. "She murdered them all and made it look like a real vampire attack so people would stop visiting Nocturnity and they'd lose their lease. She wanted the whole building to herself. My guess? Someone who didn't like what she did gave her a taste of her own medicine."

His expression never changed. "Can you prove any of that?"

"Let me out," I said. "I can prove it to you, but only to you.

No one else here would understand."

"And I will?"

"I hope so," I said. "Otherwise, Daniel and Lily Fitch are as good as dead."

"Who's Lily Fitch?"

"Long story," I said. "She's a friend."

"What about what else has been going on? With Norman and the rest of it. What's that all about?"

"Fine," I said. "I'll tell you. But you're not going to like any of it."

Without a word, Menold turned and walked out of the holding cell area. Left me there to rot. I slumped down on the bench with my head in my hands. I couldn't blame him for not believing me. Hell, I wouldn't have believed any of it either only a few years ago. Sometimes, I still had trouble believing any of it. But it was true. All of it. And more so, Lily and Daniel were lost because of me.

A loud buzzer sounded somewhere in the cell and the door clanked open. Menold stood in the doorway with a manila envelope in one hand and his keys in the other.

"This had better be good," he said. "And I want to know it all. The truth, you got me?"

I nodded.

"It's all bullshit."

Menold wove through Pittsburgh traffic like a Zen master.

"You told me you'd give me the truth."

"I did," I said. "I swear. All of it."

"C'mon. Book of the dead? Vampires? Monsters and ghosts? You're full of shit."

"I can prove it."

"Bullshit."

I shook my head and faced the window. It was a miracle he didn't turn around and take me back to jail. Had I been in his place, I might've.

"Okay," he said. "You can prove it, so prove it. How?"

"You'll see," I said. We rode in silence the rest of the way to the shop. When we pulled up in front, Menold threw the car into park.

"You got one chance to convince me," he said. "After that, if I'm not convinced, you go down."

"Are you sure?" I leveled what I hoped was warning look at him. "Once you know this, you can't un-know it. You'll see it everywhere and if you talk about it, everyone you know will treat you like you treat me."

"Whatever," he said. "Get on with it."

I shrugged and got out of the car. It was a little after two in the afternoon, and the sun still warmed the sidewalk. The front windows were unbroken and dark, as usual. I motioned for him to follow me through the door.

"Andi?" I called out for two reasons. First, I wanted to make sure she was alright. Second, I wanted to make sure I didn't surprise her. She was already hungry and on edge. The last thing I needed was for her to accidentally eat me.

"Stan!" She rushed through the beaded curtain. "Thank the Goddess! I thought—" She stopped when she caught sight of Menold. "What's *he* doing here?"

"We need as many allies as we can get, right?" I moved behind the counter and retrieved my backpack. Everything was where I left it. My eyes met Menold's one more time as if to ask him if he was sure he was sure, then I donned an oven mitt and pulled the book out.

"Here," I said. "Just like I promised. If your lab boys were to run a test on it, they'd find it's skin and blood, just like I said."

"Okay," he said. "That doesn't prove anything."

I nodded. Step two.

"How's our girl doing?" I said to Andi.

"She's better. Still a little low, but she's improving."

"Shop?" I needed to remember to give her a name. A real, decent, proper name. "It's warm in here. Could you?"

A cool breezed blew through the room and dropped the temperature by a couple of degrees.

271

"Big deal," said Menold. "You've got voice-control on your thermostat. So what?"

"I saved the best for last," I said. "C'mon."

Menold followed me to the back room. At the basement door, I stopped. As I cracked the door open, the smell hit us like a wet t-shirt to the face.

"Jesus," he snarled as he covered his nose.

I motioned for him to follow and we descended. Once in the basement, I turned to him.

"Last chance," I said. "You see this, your world changes for good."

"Thrill me," he said.

I shrugged.

"Okay. Come on out."

The vampire wasn't actually feral, as I originally thought, just horribly abused. He was kept hungry, made mean. When I called out to him, he slunk out of the darkness and stood before us. There was no mistaking his form, his translucent skin, the jagged teeth or the eyes that burned like coals.

"Holy shit," said Menold. "That's... That's a..."

"Vampire," I said. "A real, honest-to-Bela Lugosi vampire. And he's what Cassiopeia used to kill all those people."

"So what happened to her?"

"Live by the vamp, die by the vamp, I guess," I said. "She

chose him over prison."

"This is incredible."

I took him by the sleeve and led him up the stairs before he tried to pet the vampire. Andi had a mug of chamomile tea waiting. He sat on one of the barstools and stared.

"It's real," he said.

"Everything is real," I said. "Ghosts. Monsters. Demons. Magick. It's all real. Everything you spent your life denying is real, whether you want it to be or not."

"What about the shop?"

"Alive," I said.

"And you?" He nodded toward Andi.

"Witch," she said. "And... other things. It's complicated."

"And you?" He turned his crumbled stone visage to me. "How do you fit into all of this?"

"Remember when I told you I saw dead people? Taylor? Yeah. I died and came back. Now I see dead people."

"And the arm?"

"Don't you remember? Heinz Field? About a year ago? Green light and all kinds of shit going on?"

"I'd almost convinced myself I dreamed it," he said. "This is too much."

"I warned you."

"Okay," he said. "What do you need from me?"

"You'll help?"

"Cooper, you're the closest thing to a goddamned super-hero I've ever seen. How could I not help you?"

Cue the music. Hand me my cape.

Between the two of them, I figured Andi and Menold would come up with some kind of intel. With Andi's computer search wizardry and Menold's legal connections, whoever was in charge of Evergreen should've been in my lap within a few quick moments. Two hours later, however, nothing.

"Whoever he is, he's well hidden," said Andi. "It's like we're chasing a ghost."

"No names anywhere in the records," said Menold as he put his phone on the counter. "The whole thing is owned by the corporation, and no one knows squat about it. This guy may as well not exist."

I wished I could say I was surprised.

"Can you find me the layout of the building at least? That's got to be a matter of public record, right? I mean, it didn't just spring up overnight, right?"

"I wouldn't doubt it if it did," said Menold.

"Got you covered," said Andi. She shifted away from her laptop and gestured. Floorplans came up on her screen.

"Good," I said. "At least we kind of know what kind of trap

I'm walking into."

"Um, we," said Andi. "You're not going by yourself."

"Look," I said. "I can't ask you to do this. Daniel's my son and Lily is... I got them into this."

"So don't ask," said Andi. "I'm coming whether you want me to or not."

"Me too," said Menold. "I'm already in it up to my neck. Why not?"

21

The role of the hero is lonely. It's a place lots of people *think* they want to be, but when the moment strikes, they realize just what a shitty position it is. In movies, the tough young Turk stands in front of the bad guy's lair and sneers up at the facade, defies the world, and has a gut made of iron because he knows he's right and there's no way he can lose. People watch the movies to watch him make no mistakes, to see him get the girl and walk away into the sunset.

Real life isn't so carefully scripted.

It was just after 9pm. The streets were, for the most part, deserted. Those who worked in the city had gone home a while ago and the ones who stayed behind knew better than to stand in front of the building next to the glass castle. There were no signs posted, no guards, but something in the air around the building let anyone who passed by know: Keep away.

I stood in the street in front and stared up at the facade.

What floor were they on? And could I get to them before anything bad happened? Or was I already too late?

Menold stood on one side with Andi on the other. It felt good to have them around. Even if they couldn't go in with me, even if they only made it to the front door, their presence let me know I wasn't alone, no matter how I felt.

"We've got your back," said Menold. Andi nodded.

I took a deep breath and shrugged my backpack higher on my shoulder, then set off across the street. The lack of traffic meant I didn't need to be careful when I crossed, but I looked both ways out of habit. At the door I turned around and waved at Menold and Andi, then I pushed the glass door open.

It wasn't locked. There were no security guards. Just an open lobby with an unmanned guard desk and a bank of steel elevators. I took the pack off and pulled the book from inside, then dropped the pack by the door. I held the book up high so whoever watched the security cameras could see it.

"I'm here," I shouted. "Like we agreed. I've got the book. Where do you want it?"

One of the elevators gave a soft ding and opened.

Under any other circumstance, no way in Hell would I get onboard an elevator in enemy territory. Get in an enclosed space where all someone had to do was drop the box? Not likely.

But Daniel needed me, and Lily needed me. I had to do

something, even if it was suicide.

I stepped onboard and the doors slid shut.

Whoever the owner of the building was liked finery. The inside of the elevator was adorned in brushed steel and black mirrors. I tried to look anywhere but my own reflection, but no matter where I looked my own eyes stared back. And in them, right beside the scars and behind my eyes, regret for a thousand mistakes, a dozen lives lost.

"Interesting, isn't it?" The voice came from a speaker in the ceiling. "No matter who rides, no one can look at themselves too long. I wonder why that is, don't you?"

I couldn't think of an appropriately snarky reply, so I said nothing.

"Take a good, long look, Mister Cooper," said the voice. "Tell me what you see."

I didn't mean to look. Really. My intention was to stare down at my feet the whole time. But even the floor reflected my own eyes back at me. So I decided to take one good look.

The eyes, someone famous once wrote, are the windows to the soul. Might've been Shakespeare or the apostle Mark, for all I know. The point is, when a person looks into another person's eyes, in theory, he can see the wheels of his mind turn. If I look into another person's eyes, his whole past is open to me, and so is every dark secret he tries to keep.

So if I were to look into my own eyes, one would think all I'd get were either things I already knew, or just a feedback loop.

My eyes locked with themselves and some sort of psychic circuit completed. Pain tore through my skull like the claws of a bear across my scalp. Every muscle in my body seized for an instant, then released and dropped me to the floor. As I hit, I caught my reflection again, and the pain hit, harder. My body hit the floor, but my mind fell into darkness. I screamed until my throat was bloody and raw.

In my mind's eye, my mother lay on her hospital bed. At her head was a stone that gave her name and date of death. Her injuries weren't dressed, and she lay in bed and writhed in pain. Doctors walked around her, but did nothing to help.

"Nothing to be done," one said. "Shame she died because of her son."

Mom called out for me to help, but I couldn't reach her.

In the bed next to her, Maggie's emaciated body lay, split from the crotch up to her sternum. Blood soaked the sheets, but she wasn't dead. She reached out for me with skeletal fingers and begged for mercy, for relief.

"Why?" she moaned. "Why'd you put this in me? Why'd you do this to our baby?"

A doctor walked past and threw a lit match onto her bed. She went up as if soaked in gasoline, and howled in agony.

In a corner, Andi crouched as a gray figure tore at her throat and fed off her. And I couldn't do anything but watch as her pale skin turned ashen and her eyes sunk further into her skull.

Everywhere I turned, ghosts of my past came out to meet me, and every one blamed me for their deaths.

I pushed back, hard. No matter how many came from behind shadowy curtains, I turned my back and fought to walk further away. After a moment, the voices quieted, and I found myself in front of a pool of light around a crib. And I already knew what I would see when I looked in.

It was Daniel, but not as he looked in real life. The baby in the crib was twisted, scaly, with cloven hooves and black eyes and jagged teeth.

"Look at him." Maggie's voice whispered in my ear. "Look what you did to him. He'll destroy the world because of you."

But it wasn't true. Maybe the demon that left my body and entered Maggie's had taken up residence in our child, maybe that part was my fault, but Maggie had nurtured the life inside her, filled it with love, had given her life so Daniel would have a choice of what to do with his. Maggie had absolved me of the sin of my existence years before, driven away the nightmares, made me realize that I was more than a collection of unfortunate accidents and tragic events. I turned to see the person who whispered in my ear. And came face-to-face with myself.

Not me as I existed in the physical world. The me I stood face to face with was harder. His hair was a little wilder, his eyes wider. The other me smiled broad and angry, a rictus grin on my face. His hands dripped crimson and tar, and the arm that was burned on me was covered in rot on him, and the rot spread.

"You're full of shit," I said. The pain in my head lessened. "I know what you are. And you're a giant lie."

The other me faltered, took a step backward.

"You're the lie I've told myself for years."

The other me's smile grew bigger, and he gestured behind me. I followed his finger to another pool of light. In it, Lily Fitch hung suspended, arms wide, crucified on a cross of air. Her abdomen was ripped open and her intestines spilled onto the floor. Rats dined on her sticky life while she gasped for breath and stared down at me.

"You'll get her killed," said the other me. "Just like you got everyone else killed. She'll die screaming your name and cursing your existence."

"No," I said. "She won't. I'll protect her."

"Like you protected Maggie?"

"Shut up."

One of the tricks I had learned a while back was that the mind is a playground that belongs to the owner. Since it was my mind, my rules applied. Which meant that everything that happened in my mind was mine to control.

I pushed my will into my dead arm and it leapt to life, blue and electric. The rictus me threw up his good arm in defense, but too late. My will punched him in his stupid-looking mouth and sent him sprawling.

"You can't intimidate me," I bellowed. "I've already been dead. I've been burned. I've been sacrificed. I've been betrayed and left to die. You think you scare me? Dream on. I've got nothing left to be scared of!"

The rictus me scrambled backward, tried to find a shadow in which to hide. But I lumbered forward, unwilling to let my advantage slip.

"You're not me," I shouted. "You're not even good enough to wear my face! Who the hell are you?"

I lashed out with my will. It struck the other me like a whip and sizzled where it touched. The other me broke apart like a shell and exploded. Pieces of self-doubt and hate flew through the air until all that was left was the being at the core.

It was me as a child. A little boy, scared and with tears in his eyes, stared back at me, miserable and alone. And I finally understood.

I put my hand out and the child took it, and as he did, his form shifted and flowed into beautiful blue, and he was absorbed into my psyche.

I blinked and was still on the elevator, only one floor past where I was.

"Neat trick," I said, and hoped whoever was at the end of my ride could hear me. "No more games. Let's get this done."

The elevator trundled upward until it reached the top floor. It shuddered to a stop, then dinged. When the doors slid open, I expected to see maybe Hell, maybe the cheesy lair of a supervillain. I was greeted instead by chrome and glass, white carpet and elegance.

Like I said. Hell.

In the middle of the room stood a slight man in a dark suit. Though he was well-groomed, he still gave the impression of a ferret.

"Good evening," he said. "My name is Albert Wendland. I believe you have something for me?"

"Where are they?"

"Safe," he said. "Where's the book?"

"I want to see them first."

Wendland let out a sigh, then pushed a button on the table next to him. A door buzzed and opened. A large bald man with a bushy beard, dressed head to toe in black, pushed Lily out into the room. In her arms, Daniel slept.

"Are you okay?"

She nodded. Tears filled her eyes.

"There," said Wendland. "You've seen them. Now the book."

"Here," I said. I put the book on the counter and took a step back. "Now let them go."

Wendland smiled.

"Wow," he said. "I didn't think you'd be so stupid. I can't believe you actually brought it with you. What's to stop me from killing you all and taking it anyway?"

"Your honor?"

Wendland's smile vanished. In its place was the cold face of a killer. He nodded at the man in black, who drew a large knife from his coat.

"How 'bout my backup plan?"

When I had dropped the backpack at the door, I figured no one would care. Hell, there was no one down there to even see me do it, and if Wendland watched from surveillance cameras, what did an empty backpack matter?

Except that it wasn't empty. It had a passenger in the form of a curious doll that looked kind of like a monkey in a sailor suit, who answered to the name of Owen.

The man in black managed to raise his knife halfway up, but before he could start a downward stroke, the air vent in the ceiling burst out, and down came Owen in a puff of dust and supernatural rage.

I'd never seen him move before. In fact, all I knew about him was that, whenever I looked, he was in a different place. But the doll plunged down and flailed his arms. Though the placid smile never left his face, there was cold mayhem in his eyes that couldn't be denied.

The man in black's surprised cry became a muted strangle when Owen's arms wrapped around his neck. The guy thrashed and swung, tried everything to get the little monkey off his back. In any other circumstance, or if I'd seen it in a movie, the scene would've sent me into convulsive laughter. But in the moment, I was torn between being horrified and awestruck. The man in black's strength faded as Owen choked him out, then he fell and the doll returned to its motionless, deceptive state.

Wendland stared at his employee.

"Meet Owen," I said. "He and I have a deal of sorts."

"It doesn't matter," said Wendland as he rushed toward the book. "I'm going to kill you all anyway."

"I don't think so," I said.

Before he could reach the book, two of the skylights exploded and glass rained from the ceiling in a hail of razors. Two terrifying shapes dropped to the floor. The first, Andi, landed with the grace of a cat about three feet in front of Wendland. The second dropped behind him. The vampire's pasty skin seemed almost reflective in the dim light, and it snarled with the promise of food.

Wendland scrambled away, arms crossed in front of his chest. He muttered as he back pedaled, then threw his head backward. Darkness poured out of his mouth and took shape.

"The syphon!" I pushed my will into my withered arm as I ran to Lily's side. I had to keep them safe, even if it killed me.

Andi and the vampire moved as if they'd sat down and worked out a plan of attack. For all I knew they had. While she ran at Wendland, the vampire ran for the syphon. As he lunged, the syphon split into three separate entities. One stayed locked in battle with the vampire. One went after Andi. Which left the third.

"Oh, shit."

I made sure Lily and Daniel were behind me, then I pumped up the power on my ethereal arm. If it wanted me, I was at least going to make it work for its supper.

For whatever reason, the syphon wasn't camouflaged like it was the first time I encountered it. Instead of a great blank space in the fabric of the world, I saw it for what it really was. The thing looked like an imploded person, desiccated, as if every ounce of moisture had been sucked out of its body. What remained appeared to be human jerky, except that it moved and kept its mouth open in a perpetual draw. And what it drew in was energy.

I rushed it and threw my will between us. I wasn't sure why I thought such a move might work. It didn't before, but I couldn't think of anything else to do at the moment. All of the energy it came into contact with flowed through it and into the umbilical cord that fed Wendland.

"They're draining us!" There was fear in Andi's voice, and I didn't blame her one bit.

Earlier, I thought it might work if I overloaded the thing, forced too much energy through the straw, but there wasn't enough energy in my body to even hope to affect Wendland. But then something occurred to me again.

Straws go both directions.

I pulled my withered arm away and jammed my other arm, my good arm into the syphon's mouth. Then I pulled. Not with my arm, but with my core, with my will.

At first, nothing happened, and I was pretty sure I had made a colossal mistake that was about to cost my life as well as that of everyone I cared about. Then I felt a trickle, just a cold splash of life against the back of my tongue, then a bit more. Wendland's eyes opened wide and a look of panic crossed his face. I pulled hard.

The rush was amazing. So much power coursed through my body it felt like my nerves were on fire. Wendland couldn't

288

keep the three syphons at the same time, so he let the other two go. The vampire fell to his knees where the other had held him while Andi slumped to the floor and gasped for breath. Both of them looked drained, though not yet dead.

I put my withered arm out and let it act as a guide for the energy I'd stolen from Wendland. It nourished them, gave them strength. The vampire stood and roared. Andi just glared. I wasn't sure which was more frightening.

Wendland cut off the connection with the syphon, but it was too late. I'd had a nice long drink from his energy wells, and I was bursting with power. As soon as his defense was down, Andi and the vampire stalked toward him.

"Get back!" he shouted. Andi stiffened at his words, but the vampire shook his head and smiled.

The moment Wendland understood, fear registered in his eyes, then his face went placid.

"Is this what you're going to do?" he sneered. "Kill me with an animal?"

"Not unless you make me," I said. Lily, with Daniel in her arms, crossed the room and stood by my side. "I just want to be left alone. I want my family left alone."

"And the book?"

"The book stays safe," I said. "If you agree, you get to go on breathing."

"You already murdered two of the highest of our order," he said. "That can't go unanswered."

"It can," I said. "And it will. Or I'll tear your organization apart piece by piece until there's nothing left."

"You're making a mistake," said Wendland. "I'm just the first in a long line who will keep coming for you."

"Someone in your organization sent me the book to start with, didn't they?" Puzzle pieces fit together and the picture was beginning to take shape. "Someone's already trying to tear your group apart, aren't they?"

"They'll fail," said Wendland.

"Last chance," I said. "Walk. Get out of my city and leave me alone."

"We've gone far past that, I think," he said. Wendland stood up and straightened his tie and coat, then held his head up.

"In that case," I said. "I'm going to need you to send a message to your superiors."

"And what would that be?"

"I didn't say you needed to be alive to send it."

I turned my back and walked toward the door. Wendland screamed as the vampire pounced. I didn't stay to watch. I'd seen enough horrible things, and his body torn to pieces wasn't a nightmare I wanted to have.

I scooped up the book as I walked out. Lily carried Daniel

and put her arm through mine. Andi picked up Owen on the way

through the door.

"Who's this?"

"Security guard," I said.

22

Daniel gurgled and sucked on his pacifier and dozed against my chest. The little harness that kept him snug on my chest reminded me a bit of the safety straps that had broken and killed me, but more secure. There was no way I would drop my son.

The only examples I had to go by were my mom, who was the most overbearing parent I could imagine, and my father, who was so very wise, but had died when I was young. It was my hope to be a good combination of the two. The only real guideline I had to go by was the love that Maggie had poured into the kid. But if love was all it took to be a decent father, I would come up aces.

The back door beeped as it opened, but I couldn't tell who it was because of the new lightproof area around the door. None of us had installed it. We came in one day and it was done. The shop liked to take care of her mother.

"It's me," called Lily from within the darkened curtains. "I brought food."

"Good," I said. "I'm starving."

"Me too," said Andi as she climbed the stairs from the basement. "Got anything in that bag for me?"

It took us a while to get our bearings on what was going on and what our new normal was going to be. Andi claimed the basement as her own, despite the smell. After a few days and a stern talking-to, the smell abated and the moisture seemed to dry up. It became her apartment.

"I hope not," I muttered. I stuck my face in the bag. Daniel squirmed at the sound. "Sorry buddy," I said.

"Let me take him," said Andi. "He needs his Auntie, doesn't he?" She scooped him out of his harness faster than I could tell her to be careful and whisked him around the room to peals of laughter.

"Are you sure?" said Lily with a slight tilt of her head. "About..."

"I trust her," I said. "With my life."

"Good enough for me," she said.

When the vampire killed Wendland, it was the last resort. I hoped he would see reason and just leave us alone. But he chose his path, and I chose mine. Menold had waited outside the building to either arrest him or call for the meat wagon. Too bad it had to be the second.

The next night, the vampire came to claim his reward. I gave him the talisman Cassiopeia used to control him. Some would probably say it was irresponsible for me to turn that thing loose on Pittsburgh without a leash, but I just couldn't stomach keeping him prisoner. Besides, if I needed to, I knew how to find him. Andi seemed to know when he was near.

An hour later, someone burned Nocturnity to the ground. Andi was out at the time, and the building was strangely empty. The police said faulty wires. I had my suspicions.

Daniel cried. Andi dashed over and passed him off to me.

"He's stinky and hungry," she said. "Auntie Andi doesn't do diapers."

"Let me," said Lily. She scooped him up and carried him to the work bench.

"Hey," said Andi. "Look, I've been thinking about this for a while, and there's something I want you to have."

She held out her hand. In it was a glass vial, filled with crimson, wrapped in silver.

"I gave this to the vampire," I said.

"It's not his," she smiled. "It's mine. I need to know you can stop me if I ever get too bitey."

"Andi..."

"I've given this a lot of thought," she said. "And I couldn't handle it if I hurt someone. Or if I hurt you. Or Daniel. I'd die. I don't want that kind of evil loose in the world."

"You're not evil," I said.

"And you're going to help me keep it that way." She pressed the talisman into my hand and smiled.

"I'll keep it safe," I said. "I promise."

Lily finished changing Daniel and handed him back to me. I clipped him to his harness and breathed in his scent. There were hints of Maggie in his hair, in his skin.

There was a point when I couldn't look at him because I knew I'd see Maggie when I did. But I didn't mind anymore. She watched over me through the eyes of my tiny son.

Lily took my hand and kissed my cheek.

"He's a beautiful boy," she said.

"Yeah," I said. "He is."

It was time to open shop.

About the Author

Scott A. Johnson is the author of ten novels, three true ghost story guides, a chapbook and a short story collection. He currently lives somewhere near Austin, Texas, with his wife, daughter, four cats, a chihuahua, a pug, and a corn snake.

For more information, look to his website at
http://www.creepylittlebastard.com

Other Books by Scott A Johnson

An American Haunting

Deadlands

Cane River: A Ghost Story

The Journal of Edwin Grey

City of Demons

Deadlands: The definitive edition

Shy Grove: A Ghost Story

The Mayor's Guide: The Stately Ghosts of Augusta

The Ghosts of San Antonio

Haunted Austin, Texas

Droplets: A Short Story Collection

The Stanley Cooper Chronicles:
       Book One - **Vermin**
       Book Two - **Pages**
       Book Three - **Ectostorm**
       Book Four - **Bitten**